The Amish Nanny

(Amish Maids Book 1)

Samantha Price

Chapter 1

But Jesus said, Suffer little children,
and forbid them not, to come unto me:
for of such is the kingdom of heaven.
Matthew 19:14

Olive Hesh pulled her green dress over her head then smoothed it down with her hands. After she placed her white, over-apron on, she ran a brush through her long, golden hair. Once her hair was free of knots, she braided and pinned it tightly, so it would fit underneath her prayer *kapp*. Today she was heading into town to meet her friends at their favorite coffee shop. Olive had a plan she intended to share with them. She thought it time they sorted their lives out and took action toward their future. None of them had found a suitable husband, so finding a job, Olive thought, was the next best thing.

"It's all going to work out. I just know it!" Olive said aloud as she tied her *kapp* strings securely. She had to convince her four friends that her idea was a good one. Olive had the same friends since the first day that they started in the community's *skul* together; their names were Claire Schonberger, Jessie Miller, Lucy Fuller and Amy Yoder. Olive was determined that they should not stay at home and wallow in self-pity while waiting to get married as every other young Amish woman did. No, their lives would be good if they never found a man to marry. With their ages varying between nineteen and twenty, it was odd that not one of them was betrothed.

Even though she'd finished all her chores for the day, Olive slipped away from the house so her mother would not see her. If Olive's mother saw that she was going out, she would find something else that had to be done, and done at once. Around midday, Olive headed straight to the barn, got on her bike and peddled quickly away from the house.

Olive's family had three buggies, but with so many people in the family, they were almost always in use; her bike was something that she could use at anytime.

The five girls planned to be at the coffee shop at 12.30 p.m. The fact that most Amish girls of their age were already married with *kinner* and running a household forced Olive to think of her plan.

The Coffee Bean was always the same. The girls had gathered there since they were old enough to go out by themselves. Back then, they had ordered hot cocoas instead of the fancy coffees they loved these days. It was the largest coffee shop in town and had the name for making the best coffee. Tables spilled out onto the sidewalk, for those who wanted to sip their coffees alfresco. The coffee shop was owned by a local *Englisch* couple and was managed by their son Dan.

Olive took a seat at their usual table overlooking the sidewalk. The girls all loved to people-watch as they spent time together.

"Waiting for your friends, Olive?"

Olive looked up to see Dan towering over her. He was tall, with fair short-cropped hair. Technically, he wasn't handsome, but he had a pleasant and relaxed manner about him. Olive was more than sure that Lucy Fuller had a small crush on him. "Hi, Dan. Yes, I'm a little early. The other girls will be here soon."

"So you'll wait for them before you order?"

"I'll have one now thanks. And I might have another later."

Dan flashed a smile. He was handsome when he smiled like that. The coffee shop was 'order and pay at the counter,' but the five girls always received special treatment from Dan, who rushed to take their orders when they arrived.

"Latte, with two shots of caramel as per usual?"

Olive nodded and watched Dan put the order through the system. It was Saturday lunchtime, and the coffee shop would soon be full. Olive hoped she wouldn't have to defend herself against people who wanted to take the chairs away from her table. She pushed the chairs in further to distract anyone from asking her if they were in use. She hated it when that happened.

Claire was the first to arrive. Her warm smile

reached her chocolate, brown eyes as she reached over to give Olive a quick kiss on her cheek.

"So what are we doing here today?" Claire asked as she sat down. "You said you had something to say?"

Olive took a deep breath and hoped that they would all think her idea was a good one. "Wait until the others get here and I'll tell you."

Claire and Olive chatted while they waited for the other girls.

One by one, the other girls arrived. They always acted as though it had been years since they'd seen each other when in reality it was only ever days.

Lucy strode in arm and arm with Amy. They looked like they had some scheming of their own going on. The last to arrive was Jessie; she was always fond of making an entrance and thrived on trying to be a little different from everyone else. And different she was with her striking green eyes and unruly, wavy auburn hair, which she battled continually to stay within her prayer *kapp*.

Dan hurried over with Olive's coffee and took

the other orders. Olive was sure that she saw Dan pay Lucy slightly more attention than the other girls, but no one else seemed to notice.

Jessie took advantage of the lull in the conversation when Dan had finished taking the orders. "What is it you've got to tell us, Olive? I'm intrigued. Do you want to start a quilting club or something along those lines? I meant to suggest that we do something of the sort."

Three girls spoke at once on their thoughts of starting a quilting club.

Olive let them carry on for a bit and listened to their suggestions, amused that it was nothing like what she had in mind.

When the conversation died down Amy asked, "Well, is that it, Olive?" When Olive shook her head, Amy asked, "Then tell us, we're all excited to know what you're thinking."

"Okay, listen up. We're done with *skul* ages ago and none of us have anything going for us right now. We aren't getting any younger and nothing is getting any cheaper. I thought it was time to take action toward our future since none of us has a prospect of marriage."

She watched each of their faces become serious. Their advancing age and the lack of men in the community was a common concern between them now. Being as old as they were, they had to support themselves at least a little, otherwise they would become a burden on their families. None of their parents were wealthy, and they each had to pull their own weight.

It was the no nonsense Jessie Miller who came straight to the point. "Okay, boss lady, what exactly is your plan? You haven't found someone who will hire all of us, have you?"

They all joked about that scenario being the perfect situation. After all, they enjoyed each other's company and they would work well together. They had been inseparable since they were little girls. The prospect of losing contact with each other made them all nervous.

"*Nee* I haven't found someone to do that, but I have an idea. I mean it's worth a shot anyway."

The plan had sounded brilliant in her mind, but now she was a little worried about how the other girls would react to it. She had to present her plan clearly.

Olive's family were farmers and had been farmers for generations. When she visited the markets days ago, the idea had come out of nowhere. After two days of research and questioning her *mudder* who had often sold wares at the farmers' market stalls, Olive was ready to tell her friends her idea.

The girls waited as Olive laid it all out for them. "The farmers' market has tons of foot traffic. Not just regular every day people, but influential folks. I mean everyone from stay at home moms to bank managers. Think of the people who would see us." Olive's words flew out of her mouth with enthusiasm, tumbling over one another.

Lucy interrupted her. "You haven't explained what we're supposed to do."

She was right; Olive had forgotten to explain the full plan. "We rent out a stall at the market for a week. Instead of selling vegetables or crafts, we sell ourselves. I mean think of it girls - we sell ourselves! We're all looking for work."

The girls all exchanged looks and then refocused on Olive. She saw the looks they shared and knew that she had to convince them to trust her. "We each need a job, but so far we've had no success. We're all good at different things, but we can all cook and clean. We advertize ourselves to let people know." Olive still saw doubt on their faces, so she said, "Jessie, I know you've been looking for housekeeping jobs. Well, this could be your chance to find someone to hire you. You go out there and be seen – we go to them."

Amy nodded in agreement with Olive and urged the others to consider her idea.

"Amy, you love children. You would be a great nanny, but you've got to get out there so people can meet you. This is a way for people to find out about Amy and the same for each of us."

Jessie cut into Olive's sales pitch. "What if the five of us all look for jobs as maids?"

Claire said. "I like it."

Olive looked at the four girls' faces. Olive hoped that this idea would be good for all of them. Was it crazy to take out a stall at the farmers' markets in the hope for them all to find jobs?

Lucy said, "I could type up resumes for everyone at the library."

"*Jah*, great idea, *denke*, Lucy." Olive smiled pleased that she could see they were warming to her plan.

Lucy pushed out her chair and stood up. "I'll see if I can borrow pen and paper from Dan and I'll make a few notes."

The slight smile on Lucy's face at having a quiet word with Dan did not escape Olive's notice.

When Lucy came back with a notepad and pen, she jotted down notes for each of the resumes. Amy added flair to each girl's information. When they left the coffee shop, each girl had a clear idea of what they were looking for and was ready to go out and find it.

They pooled their money and rented the stall for the week.

Chapter 2

I have not hid thy righteousness within my heart;
I have declared thy faithfulness and thy salvation:
I have not concealed thy lovingkindness
and thy truth from the great congregation.
Psalm 40:10

When the first day of their week at the farmers' market came, they were all excited. They had decided beforehand to break up the week into shifts and have two people on the stall at all times. Olive was there the first day. Even though they each wanted jobs as maids, each girl had special skills. Claire was a brilliant cook, Amy was good with children, Jessie loved to garden and Claire and Lucy had experience with the sick as they had both taken care of sick, elderly relatives.

The day was warm, so they had packed along water and snacks to sustain themselves throughout the day. It was just the beginning, but from the positive input they were getting Olive knew it had been a good idea. Their individual resume flyers were being scooped up and the first reaction from passers by was positive.

The end of first day loomed near. They had handed out dozens of flyers, but so far none of the girls had found a definite job. Two hours before closing, Olive's *daed* dropped by.

"Don't look so down, Olive. It's a good sign that no one has offered to employ any of you yet. It only means that people are taking you seriously and thinking long and hard about what each of you have to offer. You've put the effort in and no effort goes unrewarded."

Olive smiled and nodded at her *daed.* He was always encouraging to his *kinner.* "*Denke, Dat,* I'm not down, I just hoped that one of us would get a job on the first day. We've got the stall for a week, and there's five us, so I was hoping that things might happen quicker."

"Always trying to force things aren't you." He put both hands on Olive's shoulders. "Let things happen in *Gott's* timing."

Olive looked back at her stall and the hopeful look on her friend's face. "Do you think that this was a bad idea, *Dat*?"

"*Nee* I don't think it was a bad idea." Olive's *daed* lowered his head and leaned toward her. "You don't need to work; we don't need the money. I want you to stay at home 'til you get married and you can help your *mudder* 'til then."

Olive frowned, she knew that things weren't as *gut* as he said; they did need extra money. "*Dat*, I don't want to move out from home, but I want to pay my way. Who knows what might happen in the future and what if I never marry? There's too many women in the community and not enough *menner*."

"Have faith, Olive."

"Okay, I will. You don't mind me getting a job though?"

He scratched his head. "*Nee*, if that's what you want to do and if your *mudder* is alright with it."

Olive nodded. "She is; I asked her."

"Do you want me to wait around for you to finish up?"

"*Nee denke.* Lucy is going to drive me home." Olive nodded toward Lucy who was speaking to an older couple stopped by the stall.

Olive's *daed* nodded and went about his business. He picked up a few things every Monday from the markets. Olive's family grew fruit and vegetables, but they needed meat, flour, cheese and milk from the markets.

* * *

None of the girls had been successful in getting a job the first day, and now it was Tuesday at two in the afternoon. Olive was growing tired of manning the stall at the farmers' market and pleased she would not have to be there the next day. Her friend Jessie was supposed to have joined her that morning, but she was nowhere in sight.

A little while later, a well-dressed lady walked past holding the hand of a toddler. The lady looked at Olive and Olive smiled at her; the lady smiled back. Olive could not keep her eyes from the handsome boy with his blonde hair. Without warning the boy grabbed resumes from Olive's stall and threw them to the ground.

"Leo, stop it, at once." The woman made a lunge for him, but the boy was too quick.

He boy jumped on Olive's papers then ran away. The woman tottered in her stiletto heels to catch up to the little boy. Olive covered her mouth in shock. She wasn't used to children who were not well behaved. Amish children were always obedient and polite. The boy turned to run the other way neatly avoiding another lunge by the older woman.

Olive stepped in front of the boy who had turned around and was now heading her way. She crouched down and said, "Hello, what's your name?"

The little boy stopped, looked into her face and poked out his tongue.

Olive ignored his antics. "Do you think you can pick up this paper faster than I can?" Olive reached out her hand to pick up the papers; the boy grabbed them up before her.

"I do it," the toddler mumbled.

"I'll do it," Olive said.

"No, me." The little boy proceeded to gather all the papers he had thrown. Once he picked up all the papers he handed them to Olive.

"Why thank you; that's very nice of you. Did you say your name was Michael?"

The little boy giggled and shook his head.

"What about David, is that your name?"

The little boy giggled again and said, "Leo."

"Oh, Leo. Well, it's nice to meet you, Leo. My name is Olive."

While Olive was still crouched on the ground, he flung his arms around her neck and nearly knocked her over and would have if she hadn't managed to grab onto the table.

The older woman grabbed the boy's arm. "Thank you, I'm terribly sorry for what my grandson has done. I don't know what gets into him sometimes."

"Full of beans they are at that age," Olive said as she stood. The little boy squirmed away from his grandmother and grabbed Olive's hand. Olive giggled. "Seems I've made a friend."

"It appears you have." The older lady stepped to one side, picked up one of the resumes and read it. "Are you looking for a job?"

"Yes, I'm looking for a job as a maid. My four friends are as well. We each have a different specialty. Are you looking for a housekeeper?"

"Well, my son, Leo's father, needs a nanny. I've told him I can't keep looking after the boy. You've seen how he is."

"My good friend Amy Yoder is good with children." With Leo still having a firm grip on Olive's hand, she used her free hand to sort through the papers to find Amy's resume.

"No, I want you for the job. You'd be perfect and in between times, you could do a little tidying up for my son."

Olive stood tall. "The only experience I've had is with my younger brothers and younger sister, nieces and nephews."

"See, that's all the experience you need. Sounds like you're a natural."

Olive wondered if this whole thing of renting

the stall at the farmers' market was a good idea after all. Was she getting in way over her head? "I do have a first-aid certificate," Olive said, more to make herself feel more qualified.

"Splendid. The job pays well and I'll make sure you're paid a week in advance. All you have to do is keep Leo occupied. You don't have to shop or clean. Blake has someone clean the house once a week and the food is delivered weekly as well."

This is all happening fast. Was she getting a real job? Could it all be this easy or would Leo's father see that she had no real experience?

"I'll write down his address. Is seven o'clock in the morning too early for you? I know he leaves for work around eight and he'll probably want to run through a few things with you." The older lady rattled around in her bag until she found a pen. She wrote down a name, address and phone number. "My name is Sonia and my son is Blake. I can't wait to tell Blake about you; he'll be so pleased that I've found a nanny."

"I'm not a real nanny though. I've got no real

experience; I just wanted a job as a maid."

"Do you want a full-time job?"

Olive quickly thought what she could do with the money from full-time employment. She could save it for her future as well as contribute to the household budget. If she never married, she did want to have her own home rather than living with one of her siblings as a sad old maid. "Full-time would be good." Leo swung on Olive's arm. "So you want me to start tomorrow?" Olive asked.

"You can, can't you? I've got a bridge game tomorrow. If I have to look after Leo again, I'll have to cancel. Then after that, I've got my hair appointment with Maxwell Leon. I've had that appointment booked for four weeks; he's so hard to get into. He's an excellent colorist." Sonia looked at Olive's prayer *kapp.* "I guess you've no need for a hairstylist."

Olive touched her fingertips to her prayer *kapp* and looked at the blonde hair piled high on Sonia's head. "Yes, tomorrow is fine," Olive said when she took the information from Sonia. Olive glanced at the paper and recognized the street name and was pleased that it wasn't too far from her home. It was close enough that she could ride her bike. "Nice and close." Olive smiled. "Are you sure this will be alright with your son? I mean he's never met me."

"It'll be okay. I make most of the decisions for him; he's so busy. He works far too much."

Leo squealed about something, let go of Olive's hand and his little chubby legs began to run. Sonia ran to grab his arm and this time she was successful. She turned back to Olive. "Thank you, Olive. I'll see you again."

"Yes. And I'll be there tomorrow. Thank you very much, Sonia."

Olive's eyes fixed upon Sonia and Leo as they disappeared down one of the laneways. Leo needed discipline; he wasn't a bad child. Olive knew that every child needed structure and discipline and it seemed to Olive that Leo lacked both of those. She wondered why Leo's mother wasn't mentioned. Were Leo's parents divorced?

An hour before the farmers' markets closed for the day, Jessie rushed toward the stall. "I'm so sorry, Olive. There was an accident, and my *bruder* broke his leg. He was fixing something on the roof, and he slipped off. He's still in the hospital."

"That's awful, Jessie. He will be alright, won't he?"

"It was a bad break, but I guess he's lucky he didn't do any more damage. A tree broke his fall."

Jessie's parents' *haus* was built over two levels, so her *bruder* would have fallen from quite a height. "You need not have come in at all, Jessie."

"I said I'd be here. I always do what I say." Jessie gave a sharp nod of her head as if to emphasize her point.

Olive touched Jessie lightly on her arm. "Do you want me to get you a cup of tea or something?"

Jessie shook her head. "I'm okay. I had too many *kaffes* in the hospital while we were waiting for the x-rays and when we were waiting for the cast. He'll be back home tonight."

"Sit down while I give you some good news."

Olive pulled a small chair out from under the table and when Jessie sat down, she told her the news of her new job.

Jessie clapped her hands. "You were right to do this. We'll all have jobs soon. I'm so pleased for you, Olive."

"*Denke.* Well, we'll have to re-arrange the schedule since it looks like I won't be here for the rest of the week."

"I'll arrange it with the others; you just concentrate on your new job. I didn't know you wanted to work with children; I thought that's what Amy wanted to do."

"I tried to tell the lady about Amy, but she said the little boy got on well with me, so she wanted me." Olive breathed out heavily.

"What's the matter? You look upset now."

"The *grossmammi* hired me, but the catch is that the boy's *daed* knows nothing of me. How do I know I'm not going to show up at the house for nothing? I might be back here after all. It's not as if the boy's *mudder* or *vadder* hired me.

Jessie drew her chin in toward her chest. "*Nee*, surely not. She would have had the 'say so' otherwise she would not have given you the job."

"I'm probably worrying about nothing. Anyway, it's not my turn on the stall tomorrow. If I go there and have to leave straight away, it doesn't matter. In a way, I've got nothing to lose." Olive noticed that Jessie's face was pale and more hair than usual was poking out from underneath her *kapp*. "You go home, Jessie. I'll be finished up soon; there probably won't be many people interested in hiring a maid this late in the day."

"I feel terrible for letting you down today, Olive."

"Nonsense. Go and look after that *bruder* of yours and make sure he stays on the ground."

Chapter 3

Wherefore, if God so clothe the grass of the field, which to day is, and to morrow is cast into the oven, shall he not much more clothe you, O ye of little faith?

Matthew 6:30

"We're home!" Sonia called out in a singsong voice as she made her way into the house. "And someone better be home because someone forgot to lock the door again."

Sonia held the door for Leo as he toddled into the house with an oversized brown bag balanced in his arms. "Well, thank you kindly, good sir! You are such a big help bringing in those vegetables for me."

Leo's face beamed in response as he looked up at her from under his blonde curls. Sonia noted it was near time for him to get another haircut. She would have to remind Blake to do that; she had done her duty long enough, looking after Leo every day for the past months.

Leo pulled out a head of corn from the bag he dropped on the kitchen floor. "Can I eat it?"

"Maybe for dinner," Sonia said. "I love some good fresh corn too. We have to cook it first though."

"Hey there!" A deep voice greeted them.

Sonia looked up to see her son striding down the hall.

"I thought I heard voices out here," Blake said.

"Only a couple vandals out to rob you while you're busy in your den with the front door unlocked," Sonia chided Blake lightly, as she gave him a peck on the cheek in greeting. "You need another pair of hands around here, honey. You're starting to get absent-minded."

"Working on that, Mom," Blake answered as he took another bag of food from his mother. Then he leaned over to take the bag his son had dumped on the floor. "How'd you do today, champ? Want me to take that?"

"No! I want it!" Leo said, hugging the head of corn as he shuffled his way quickly out of the kitchen.

Blake watched him run away. "He looks tired. What did you two get up to today?"

"Leo made a friend at the farmers' market." Sonia chuckled at Blake's perplexed expression. "He got a few good words of wisdom from a very nice lady. She was a young lady and pretty too. I think it was good fortune for both of us that we happened to go there today."

"Sorry to have Leo joining you on errands, Mom. I'm working to find him a good nanny as soon as possible. Now, I know that you said you'd look after him, but I know it hasn't been easy. I can see the tension on your face."

"Oh, don't worry your mind on that. I have loved having him with me." Sonia waved his comments away. "Since you've just brought up the subject of a nanny, I've got some great news for you."

"That so? The markets have a good special today? I know how you love bargains," Blake said only half listening to his mother as he went in search of where Leo had run to with the corn.

"Oliff!" Leo crowed triumphantly as he ran out from his bedroom towards his father.

"Oliff? What's he trying to say, Mom? He's been speaking so clearly lately now he's back to the baby-talk." Blake's eyes widened slightly and he caught himself with a relieved smile. "Oh, you bought olives at the store. I love olives."

"No!" Leo said, looking at his dad with a very familiar impatient expression. "Oliff, lady."

"Yes. We found a lady called Olive at the markets didn't we, Leo." Sonia beamed as she took off her soft, leather jacket. "Now, I think it's time for the cartoons, isn't it?"

"Mom, you know I don't like him sitting in front of the television all day."

The diamonds on her fingers flashed as Sonia waved a manicured hand in the air. "It won't hurt for a little bit. I've got something to tell you and I can't tell you while Leo's screaming the house down." Sonia turned to her grandson. "Cartoons, Leo?" Leo made a dash for the living room.

"Oh, no." Blake managed to beat Leo to the

remote for the flat screen, saving it from smudges of sticky fingers.

Once the television was set with cartoons and Leo sat transfixed by the colorful characters, Blake walked toward his mother. Sonia was busy putting away the vegetables. She smiled when she looked up to see Blake's worried face.

"What do you have to tell me, mother?"

"Before you get angry, just hear me out. I hired a nanny, and she starts tomorrow."

"What? You what?" Blake collapsed heavily onto one of the stools pushed up against the granite kitchen island. "Why so suddenly; couldn't we have talked about this first?"

Sonia turned, shut the refrigerator door and put one hand on her hip. "Do try to be more open-minded, Darling."

Blake glared at her through narrowed eyes. "Please tell me that you're joking."

"You're just like your father when you look at me like that."

"What's wrong with my father?"

Sonia rolled her eyes. "Don't get me started on that one. Anyway, you should have seen Olive with Leo. He was throwing things, jumping on things and running away and with a few quiet words from her, he turned into an angel. Did I mention that she was attractive? When I found out she was looking for a job, it was obvious what the next step had to be.

"Was it?"

"Of course, Darling. It simply made sense that she was the perfect person to look after him. Someone has to manage him. I know you believe in him being a free spirit, but he needs firmness."

"I know he needs firmness. When I said I wanted him to be able to think for himself I meant when he was older. I don't know where you got the free spirit nonsense from I never said that, not once."

"He takes after you. You were a handful too when you were his age. I thought I could manage him every day and I want to, but I can't. I've things to do and putting it simply, a grandson does not fit in with my lifestyle." She watched Blake's expression. "At this stage of my life, I'm entitled to some *me* time."

Blake leaned on the kitchen island and rubbed his forehead. "I said it would be too much for you. Thank you for trying, it means a great deal to me. But, you could have let me find a nanny."

"Do you have coffee made?"

"Wait a minute. Who is this person you hired?" Blake asked. "You always do this, Mother. You always decide what's best for me without even asking me. Why couldn't you have waited and asked me about it first?"

"You would have said no." Sonia's tone was cheerful and matter of fact, despite her son's glowering expression. "Now, your new nanny is a lovely young lady called Olive Hesh."

Blake suppressed a sigh of exasperation. "The agency sent me loads of resumes, over a month ago. I could have chosen one of them."

"Leo and I hired one for you. Problem solved!" Sonia smiled as she checked the coffee pot. "I know you were set on finding a perfect caretaker but as it turns out, she found us. It really couldn't have worked out more perfect."

"Mom, I wish you would have checked with me first. I can't have someone I've never met look after Leo. I'll have to phone her and tell her not to come, but I could have her come for an interview first."

"Yes, yes, but then you'll put the whole thing off. It would have taken over a year with you being the perfectionist that you are." Sonia poured two cups, waving him off as he tried to take over. "I've got this, sit back down. Come on now and relax. She is perfect for the job. You will love her. I guarantee it."

* * *

Blake took a slow breath. There were moments where his mother went too far with her controlling ways even if well intended. "Would you please start at the beginning? Where did you meet this woman? What are her qualifications?"

His mother took a sip of coffee. "Leo and I were at the market as I said. And he started into a fit about something or other. He was trying to drag me off to see something that he'd spotted. I thought we would have to leave he was making such a scene. People were staring." Sonia raised a finger to stop Blake as he opened his mouth. "Don't start on his behavior, we're talking about something more important at the moment."

Blake nodded and kept quiet.

"Anyway, this darling young lady came over and started talking to Leo. She crouched down and chattered with him about how boring shopping can be and asked him what his name was. I couldn't really hear too much of what they were talking about, but he took to her instantly. He was an angel the rest of our trip."

"She works there? So, she runs a fruit stall or some such stall and you think she's capable of looking after Leo?"

"Now don't huff and puff so. She explained to me that she and a couple of friends were out of

33

work and they set up a stall to advertize themselves in the hope of finding employment."

"How industrious of them."

"Exactly what I thought. It shows that they're hard working and you have to admire their resourcefulness."

"I don't need entrepreneurial skills; I just need a nanny. Please tell me she has some experience at least. Was she looking to get a job in childcare?"

"She was looking for a job as a housekeeper."

Blake pressed his lips together. He didn't want to get too angry with his mother; she was genuinely trying to help. She would truly believe that the girl would do a good job.

"Leo doesn't usually take to people so quickly. So I asked if he wanted her to look after him and he said yes. I did ask him after I asked her, of course."

Blake gasped and sputtered, ignoring the coffee that was growing cold in front of him. "Mother, I'm trying very hard not to get angry. I can't get my head around the idea that you hired a strange woman that neither of us know, just because she spoke nicely to Leo."

"Oh, it was much more than that. I have a good feeling about this one. She will be an absolute dream. Don't worry about the salary. I'll be paying her, so don't fret about the wages."

"No, Mother. I can afford to hire a nanny for my own son."

"And fire them?" Sonia asked with a knowing smile. "Relax, Darling. You can take over her salary after she's been here a while if you like. But, I know you well enough not to leave her in your hands with fifty excuses not to even try."

"I'll need my police friend, Doug Briggs, to run a background check on her. What's her name again?"

"Blake James William Worthington, you'll do no such thing. You can't do something like that without asking a person. Anyway, she told me she has many brothers and sisters who she looked after. I think it was six she said she had. Maybe four or could have been six younger brothers and sisters. You can't get better on the job training than that.

Those ninnies you're looking over in those resumes might never have changed a diaper in their lives. You can't learn about kids from a classroom and an exam. Papers don't give you a personality either."

"Mother, this is insane. I will not choose a nanny on someone's personality. I hope you didn't either."

"It's what people have done for hundreds of years. Find a nice woman who knows kids and hires them. It's not that difficult, dear. Millions of children have survived the process." She smiled in that calm, stubborn way that told Blake that no matter what he said or did, the matter was settled. Nothing would change her mind or stop Sonia from having her way on this one.

"Trust me, dear. I have a great feeling about this one. Mother knows best."

"Right," Blake grumbled. He took a sip of his coffee, which had grown cold. He hoped this new excuse for a nanny would not prop his son in front of the television all day.

His mother meant well, but how would he go to work tomorrow knowing that a stranger with minimal experience would be in charge of the most precious person in his life? It was absurd.

Chapter 4

And Jesus said unto them, Because of your unbelief:
for verily I say unto you, If ye have faith
as a grain of mustard seed,
ye shall say unto this mountain,
Remove hence to yonder place;
and it shall remove; and nothing
shall be impossible unto you.
Matthew 17:20

E ven though she had a day's work ahead of her, Olive did her fair share of chores before she left the house.

Olive rode her bike directly to the address she had been given by Sonia, and when she arrived, she looked up at the house and double-checked the address. She had the right house, but she hadn't expected the house to be quite so grand. She climbed off her bike, wheeled it to the side of the house and leaned it against the wall.

It all made sense; it appeared that Sonia's son

was just as wealthy as his mother. Even at the farmers' market she was covered in diamonds and no doubt designer clothes. They had to be wealthy for Sonia to offer the kind of money she mentioned yesterday.

The yard was beautifully landscaped and looked as if it was a park rather than a private yard. Olive wondered if Sonia's son took care of it himself or whether he had a gardener. No, Sonia mentioned that her son worked all the time, so he most likely employed a gardener. It had to take a considerable amount of time to keep the flowerbeds and hedges in such exact and pristine shape.

Sonia had made no mentioned of Leo's mother, so Olive consider that her son was most likely divorced or was a widower.

The reality of her new job had Olive's heart pounding in her ears as she hesitated at the backdoor. *Keep it together, Olive.* Steadying herself with a deep breath, she pressed the doorbell.

It seemed that this man, Blake, wanted his mother to look after his young boy, but Sonia had other priorities. Olive giggled to herself about Leo's behavior the day before; she was used to young children and knew how to distract them. She had a theory that children only misbehave to gain attention.

After a reasonable amount of time had past she pressed the doorbell again. After there was still no response she called out, "Hello?"

"Come in," she heard a male voice say from somewhere within the house.

She opened the door, walked in and looked around about her and saw no one. She walked further inside, and her breath caught in her throat when she saw the kitchen. It looked as though it was straight from one of the designer magazines she often flipped through at the coffee shop. It was all dark wood and glossy, with white stone counter tops and gleaming stainless steel appliances.

She secretly couldn't wait until she could cook something in there. Olive snapped out of it and wondered where Leo and his father were. Olive moved through the house silently towards Leo's squeals to see that they were coming from the next level. She stopped at the bottom of the wide staircase when she heard Leo's feet come padding down.

"Leo, Leo, stop running!" Blake yelled from behind his son.

Olive moved quickly to intercept the little boy when he reached the bottom of the staircase. She held her arms out wide and scooped him up. Leo squealed louder as she swung his little body around in a circle. She was so distracted by his happy smiling face that she momentarily forgot about the boy's father.

Blake stood at the bottom of the staircase and looked her up and down. "I'm sorry; I thought you were someone else. I'm not interested in any religious chatter, and I'm getting ready for work." Blake motioned toward the door. "I'll walk you out."

Olive opened her mouth in shock. "Didn't your mother mention me?"

With raised eyebrows he said, "You're the

nanny?"

"Yes." Olive relaxed the tension that had suddenly built up in her shoulders. Sonia had told him that she was coming.

"You're Amish," he said in an accusatory tone.

Olive smiled at him. "Yes, I am."

"And you're my mother's idea of the perfect Nanny?"

"She said that?" Olive tried to pay attention to Leo and Blake at the same time.

Blake crossed his arms and studied her through narrowed eyes. He couldn't have made it more obvious that she was not welcome.

She ignored his wariness and put out her hand. "Hello, I'm Olive Hesh."

His handshake was firm and his skin was velvet soft, not like the harsh blistered hands of most of the Amish farm boys she knew.

"Blake Worthington, and I understand you're already acquainted with my son."

"I do hope it's alright me being here. Sonia seemed quite pleased to have me watch Leo." She felt a clench of anxiety at his doubtful expression. It was clear that he did not share his mother's enthusiasm, which caused Olive's smile to falter.

Relief washed over her as Blake said, "You're early. Sorry about before, but I've never had much to do with the Amish. When I saw you just inside the door I thought you'd come to save me from – well, save me from myself."

Olive felt heat rise in her cheeks. "We don't push our beliefs onto others. And I'm sorry if I caught you at a bad time. I always try to be a little early. It's a habit that I got from my mother; she always has to be ten or fifteen minutes early wherever she goes."

"No," he said, "I like people to be on time. People don't value time nowadays. I subscribe to the notion that time is money."

"I know what you mean." Olive relaxed enough to notice that he was a handsome man and so tall that he towered above her.

Sonia didn't say what her son did for a living, but he did not have the build of an office worker.

His hard body resembled someone who worked hard for a living, such as a farmer or a construction worker. He wore a white, business shirt and dark, gray suit pants, so it seemed his job was an office job of sorts. It was not the time to ask him what kept him away from his son for so long every day.

"Olive, I need to talk to you about this arrangement."

"Ollie, Oliff!" Leo cheered as he wrapped himself around her in an excited hug before grabbing her hand to drag further into the house. "Let's play! Come see my room!"

"I'd love to!" Olive knelt down, so she was eye to eye with the boy. "But first I need to talk to your daddy for a moment. Would you be a dear and set up the first game you want to play while he and I talk?"

"I wanna play with you now," Leo said, his voice lilting upwards into a whine.

Blake frowned and gently laid a hand on his son's shoulder and opened his mouth to speak, but Olive was quick to say, "Grown-ups talk first and

45

then we play. Now you wait for me in your room."
Olive's tone was firm but nice.

Leo turned and toddled slowly to his room.

Blake watched his son walk away. "That was well done. He does listen to you."

Olive stood up. "You wanted to speak to me?"

"Yes, come and sit in the kitchen."

While they sat, Olive studied his face. His jawline was strong, his nose was nicely shaped and not too big and his lips were full but masculine. His eyes were as dark as his hair and his face was clean-shaven. After Blake still hadn't said anything, Olive asked, "What was it that you wanted to speak to me about?"

"Oh, yes." He coughed and glanced at the clock. "I want to make it clear that this is temporary. A trial run if you will. You'll be paid of course."

She nodded. "Yes, Sonia, um, your mother, made it clear yesterday."

"She gave me to understand she said nothing of a trial period."

Olive did not want to get his mother into trouble

and by the frown on Blake's brow it looked as though that was in danger of happening. "I was a little distracted by your beautiful son and his beautiful, fair hair. I don't fully remember the exact conversation."

Blake's face softened, and he gave a low chuckle. "His hair used to be long and curly, but we had to have it cut because everyone thought he was a girl. He can be quite distracting. Everyone makes such a fuss of his blonde hair that I think Leo is certain he can get away with anything."

"I assure you I won't let him misbehave. My parents were quite strict and firm, but fair." Olive gave a quick nod of her head.

Blake's lips turned upward at the corners. "And how old are you? Normally, I wouldn't ask a lady her age, but I guess I'm entitled to know in circumstances such as these."

Olive tilted her chin upward. "I'll be twenty soon, Mr. Worthington."

He visibly winced and shook his head. "Blake, just Blake, please. I always think people are referring to my late father when they call me Mr. Worthington."

"Sorry." She gave him a smile. "I can't promise I'll always catch myself though. It tends to be a habit. My family is old fashioned when it comes to respecting elders."

"Heavens, I'm not that old."

"Sorry." She lowered her head hoping that she would not have to watch what she said every single day.

"Nothing wrong with respect," he affirmed as he checked his watch once more. "I'm trying to get Leo on a schedule, but Mom's let that slip by the wayside. I think he needs a set schedule. The emergency contact numbers are on the fridge." He stood up. "I'll show you where Leo's room is before I go to work."

"Yes, Mr. Worthington, I mean, Blake," she corrected herself in a quick breath. He stared at her as she gave him a light apologetic look. "I did say it was a habit!"

"I'm sorry if I appeared to be a little short with

you earlier. I was shocked that my mother employed a nanny on my behalf without prior discussion. I can't make any promises to keep you on, but since you're already here, maybe you could just look after him today?"

Olive was confused; didn't he just say he'd give her a short trial period? "Sonia assured me this would be a full-time position. I understand that you might want to give me a trial period of say, two weeks?"

Blake breathed out heavily and put his fingertips to his forehead, covering his eyes as if he had a headache coming on. "Very well, very well. Two weeks and see how we all work together."

"I've done a first aid course." Olive hoped that would make him happy.

"And I'm assuming my mother looked at your references?"

"Oh, I've never done this before, but I've got a lot of brothers and sisters and lots of nieces and nephews."

Blake rolled his eyes and shook his head while

his face turned a shade of red. "That woman... You mean you've got no references, at all?"

Olive shook her head and wondered if she would have to turn around and ride all the way home again.

There was no more talk of references or Blake's mother as Blake quickly showed her the bathroom, a couple of the spare bedrooms and Leo's room. The last room they came to was Leo's.

Leo sat on the floor playing with toy trucks. "Ollie, play now?"

Blake ignored his son, looked at his watch and then looked down at Olive. "Coffee, I need coffee. Can you at least make coffee?"

Olive hesitated. Had he made up his mind already that he was not going to be satisfied with her performance? "Yes, I can. Come with me, Leo; we can play later and now you can help me fix your daddy coffee."

Leo jumped up and down and followed Olive into the kitchen.

Minutes later, Blake appeared in the kitchen

tying his tie.

"How do you have it?" Olive asked quite distracted by a man getting dressed in front of her.

Blake sat on a stool. "Just black, no sugar."

Olive placed the coffee in front of Blake then picked Leo up and balanced him on her hip. "He's only got underpants and socks on. I'll go and dress him."

Blake waved a large, tanned hand in the air. "Yes, then come straight back so I can speak to you. I've got to leave soon."

"Oh, do you want me to cook you some breakfast?"

Blake shook his head. "No need. I always eat out."

Olive nodded and made her way upstairs with Leo.

"And don't let him talk you into playing before you come back," Blake called after them.

Olive looked into the little boy's face and whispered to him, "You've gotten us in trouble before breakfast." The boy laughed and buried his face into her shoulder. They climbed the tall staircase and made their way into Leo's room.

Leo's room was filled with toys and Olive considered that he could give two-thirds away to the poor and still have more toys than he would ever play with. "I've never seen so many toys except in a toy store." She set him down and dressed him ready for the day. She slipped a soft, yellow shirt over his head and snapped his overall clasps at his shoulders. She examined the stitches on the overalls and knew that they must have cost a sum. The overalls were double-stitched and fully lined with a different fabric. *Humph, a far cry from Amish hand-me-downs.* As she tied his sneakers, Leo played with the strings of her prayer *kapp*.

"Hungry now, Ollie. Gimme some berries."

Olive laughed at how cute her name sounded when he tried to say it. "Leo, you should say, can I have some berries, please?"

"Can I have some berries, peeees?" Leo said with a sweet smile displaying his tiny white baby teeth.

"No, I can't give you berries. I will give you something, but let me finish here first." Leo wound the strings of her prayer *kapp* around his fingers while she finished tying his left shoelace.

"Hungy, Ollie," Leo said with his voice raised.

She laughed at his demands and begged him once more to say please. He did and then jumped into her waiting arms.

Olive knew she would like playing with Leo every day; he was such a happy child and full of life. All she had to do now was prove to Blake that she was the right person for the job. They headed down to breakfast and now she would be able to hear what Blake wanted to say to her. Olive settled the little boy into his booster seat and set out to make some breakfast for him.

Blake stopped her in her tracks. "What are you doing?"

Olive was half in the refrigerator when he spoke to her. She leaned back out with a bowl of strawberries in hand. "I'm making breakfast for Leo."

He stormed to the other side of the large, kitchen island and yanked a sheet of paper off the top. Blake shoved the paper in front of her. Olive tried to read what was on the paper, but he kept moving it.

"Blake, you're making me sick in the tummy with moving the paper. What exactly is on it?"

He huffed out a breath and slammed the paper down on the island. "It's the rules and instructions for the day. Including that berries sometimes cause him to get a rash. It also states what breakfast is supposed to be. I don't think that this is a good idea. I don't think that you're mature or experienced enough for this job. Not that my mother cares at all what I think. I did also say that I wanted to speak with you. I assumed you would give me your full attention rather than make Leo breakfast."

Leo ignored the tension in the room; all he wanted was berries. "Ollie, berries pwease!"

Olive took the berries out of Leo's cereal and went to take it to him, but Blake was standing in her way.

Olive and Blake stared at each other for a minute before he stepped aside to let her pass. Leo was clapping in happiness at the sight of his food. She placed the bowl on the table in front of him and turned back to Blake. "You're quite right, Blake, I'm sorry. I was distracted by his hunger. What do you want to say to me?"

Olive noticed his face was red as he said, "What's the point? My mother's taken over my life once again."

Before they had a chance to discuss the list again, Blake kissed little Leo goodbye and asked her to follow his instructions. Then he was gone.

Blake had a lot of instructions, but Olive didn't mind.

Even though he had checked the time every five minutes, Blake complained of being late. Was he late or did he just want to get away from her and the reminder of his mother taking over his life?

Chapter 5

My brethren, count it all joy when ye
fall into divers temptations;
Knowing this, that the trying of your
faith worketh patience.
But let patience have her perfect work,
that ye may be perfect and entire, wanting nothing.
James 1:2-4

When he was well clear of the house, Blake called his mother determined to deliver some stern words. What did she think she was doing to saddle him with a mere girl, an Amish girl at that? How could she possibly be capable of looking after his son?

Finally, his mother answered the phone.

"Mom, you didn't tell me she was Amish."

"I didn't think it relevant. If anything it makes her more trustworthy. The Amish have big families and she's come from a big family; she told me so herself."

"You could have warned me that's all. When I saw her walk through the door, I thought she was peddling her religion."

Sonia laughed and then quickly said, "I hope you weren't rude to her."

"Of course not." Blake made a quick end to the conversation and turned his attention back to the road. What did he think he would achieve by speaking to his mother? She had never listened to him in the past. She thought she knew what was best for him and his life. Nothing he did had ever stopped her being controlling. Blake put it down to him being an only child. If he'd had siblings then her attention would have been less focused on him.

That morning he had hoped to turn the new nanny away politely and pay her for the trouble of coming there. But since she was there and Leo seemed pleased to see her, he had relented. When he saw how Olive thwarted one of Leo's tantrums, he thought she deserved a trail period. Now, he was annoyed with himself. It was just another win for his mother and her meddling ways.

Leo needed more than a young nanny; he needed someone to guide him before his behavior became unmanageable. Blake knew that his work kept him away too often to provide the structure that Leo needed. *Olive's a pretty girl; it's a shame she's hidden away from the world living with the Amish. She's got a natural warmth and friendliness. I hope she did not take offense at my reaction to her. It's not her fault that she was swept up into my mother's scheming ways. I should apologize to the poor girl.*

* * *

Olive picked up Blake's list of instructions for Leo sorting through what was important and what was not. There were far too many things on the list to remember by heart and Olive wanted to follow the most essential. By midday, she and Leo were still getting along fine.

She decided to do something special for lunch. Olive prepared peanut butter and jelly sandwiches, carrot sticks, a couple of water bottles and loaded them into a small cooler she had found in the laundry. Along with an oversized picnic rug, Olive found a small ball and placed them in Leo's old pram that she found in the utility room. They were going outdoors into the fresh air and the park down the road was the perfect place. Leo refused to get into the pram, so Olive placed all the goods inside it rather than carry everything and let Leo walk.

She and Leo had a picnic lunch in the sunshine. After lunch, she pushed the little boy on the toddler swing and then chased him around the park until he exhausted himself. She set up the large rug under the shade of a large willow tree and settled Leo on her lap.

Olive pulled out one of his books and read aloud. It didn't matter what the story was the key was the tone of her voice. Olive read aloud until Leo's breathing slowed and he drifted off to sleep.

They stayed in the shade of the tree while Leo had a nap. Olive couldn't remember the last time she had felt this happy or this at peace. Her mind wandered as she felt Leo's warm breath fan across her skin. Her thoughts turned to Blake; he was a mystery to her. He seemed so angry, but why? She remembered the look on his face that morning as he watched her make the breakfast. It had broken her heart that he showed his anger in front of his young son.

Her eyes drifted to the little boy in her lap. Leo looked so much like his dad except for Leo's light hair. They were both so handsome, so... Olive shook the thought right out of her head. She had no business thinking about Blake being attractive. She was the nanny and Blake was not even a suitable match for her being an *Englischer* and all. Just in age alone, Blake must have had over a decade on her.

A cold wind started up, so Olive shut down all thoughts of Blake and gathered their belongings. Once everything was packed away, Olive picked up the still sleeping boy into her arms and placed him in the pram. Now, she was especially thankful she had brought the pram; she would never have been able carry him home. She covered Leo with the blanket and quickly walked back to the house.

When they arrived home, Leo woke. They enjoyed the rest of the afternoon while they waited for Blake's return. Olive felt a sense of satisfaction that she had made it through the first day.

It was ten minutes past six when Olive heard Blake's car in the driveway. She had no idea what hours she was supposed to work and was glad that her mother offered to keep her dinner aside for her. Leo and Olive were playing with a train-set to the side of the living room when Blake's key jiggled in the lock.

Leo sprang to his feet just as Blake stepped through the door. "Daddy, daddy."

Blake picked him up.

Olive stood up and smoothed down her dress. "Hello, we've had a lovely day."

"Well, I haven't; I'm tired and I'm not in the best of moods." He walked a few steps and threw his keys down on a side-table. "Look, I'm sorry about this morning. I had no idea that my mother would employ a nanny. She said that she could look after

Leo herself. I told her it would be too much for her, but she had insisted. You can understand my shock when she came here yesterday to tell me she hired a nanny."

Olive scratched her neck. What did he want her to say? They had discussed all that earlier in the day. Whenever she got nervous, she broke out into a rash, and she did not like to have confrontations with people. "I understand it might frustrate you, but I'm here to help."

Blake nodded. "I appreciate it," he said as he sat down on the couch still holding Leo. "What did you do today, Leo?"

"We wen to da park," Leo said.

"You did?" He looked over at Olive. "It's far too cold for the park in this weather."

"It was warm when we started out, but we came back before it got too cold. Before that though, we had a picnic, played on the swings and then Leo fell asleep."

"Fell asleep? He never has naps in the middle of the day. Miss Hesh, that simply won't do; you must try to keep him awake. Now, he won't go to sleep until past midnight. None of us will get any sleep."

Her hand flew to her mouth. "I'm so sorry." She hadn't given one thought to his sleep routine.

"Didn't you read my list? It was on the list. If I knew you would not read the list I would not have bothered writing it."

"I'm so sorry; I was distracted. I read it through once, but just quickly."

His dark eyes bore through her. "A proper nanny would realize that you have to keep children to a strict routine."

Olive looked away. She couldn't disagree with what he said, but why did he have to speak so harshly?

"Has he had his bath, at least?" Blake's face was hard, like stone.

"Yes, he's had his dinner and his bath."

As Blake looked back to Leo, he said, "At least that's something I suppose."

Olive was annoyed with herself. He'd given

her the list, why hadn't she taken more notice of it? "I'll take the instructions home and read them through."

"Home? You mean you're not live-in?"

"No; your mother said nothing about being live-in." Olive frowned; she was not sure how the bishop would react to her living in the house of a single *Englisch* man. *Nee*, it would not be approved. "I can't do that; I'm sorry."

"I assumed you would, I mean that's what a nanny does, I thought. Anyway, it's late, how will you get home?"

"I've got my bike outside."

He looked her up and down. "Amish may ride bikes and not drive cars?"

Olive nodded. "It's a push bike. What time do you want me to start and finish each day? That is if you still want me to work here."

Blake scratched his head. "I'm prepared to give it two weeks and see how we go. Be here at eight. I vary the times I finish, so can you be here 'til I come home?"

Olive nodded. "Yes, I can do that."

Leo gave a big yawn.

"Looks like you might get some sleep," Olive said smiling at Leo's tired face.

Blake looked down at his son. "He looks a little sleepy."

"Good night, Leo. I will see you tomorrow."

Leo looked up at her and smiled sweetly.

Olive rose to her feet. "Good night, Blake."

"Thank you for today, Olive. I hope I didn't make things too difficult for you. My mother keeps telling me my temper is getting worse."

Olive tingled inside on hearing Blake say her name. "Not at all," she said speaking in the most business-like tone she could muster.

"I also must apologize again for my reaction to you being Amish. It was just that I thought my mother would have told me."

"She most likely considered that it wasn't a factor as it wouldn't affect my looking after Leo."

Blake frowned a little and avoided eye contact with Olive. "Yes that would be it."

Olive left the house and walked to her bike relieved to be getting away from Blake and his temper. She reminded herself that it was just the first day, and it was natural that it would be a difficult one. Her mother had taught her to look at the other person's point of view in every situation. As she rode her bike down the street, she considered things from Blake's point of view. He was forced into having a nanny and it wasn't even a nanny that he had chosen. No wonder he was cranky.

Chapter 6

Blessed is the man that endureth temptation:
for when he is tried,
he shall receive the crown of life,
which the Lord hath promised to them that love him.
James 1:12

A few days along, Olive thought Blake would have gotten used to her looking after Leo. He had apologized for his rudeness several times.

Every morning, when she arrived, it was the same thing; Blake greeted her with a list of things from the day before that she could've or should've done better. She did not understand why he disliked her so much; she tried her best to do her job, but Blake always found some reason to scold her.

After another early morning reprimand, she heard the screeching tyres of his car as it sped away. She wanted to shout at him at times, but she loved looking after Leo and she appreciated the wages.

She walked upstairs to get Leo out of his pajamas

and change him into his day clothes.

Olive heard a key jiggle in the front door and then heard, "Olive, will you come down? I need to talk to you, dear." It was Sonia Worthington. Sonia had called in every day to see how she was getting along with Blake. Olive had found out that she was not the only one who found Blake hard to get along with.

"I'm just dressing Leo; I will be right there." Olive tried her best to control her shaking voice. She wiped the tears and checked herself in the mirror; Mrs. Worthington should not see she had been crying.

She came downstairs to see Sonia sitting at the kitchen table.

"Come here my dear sit down with me," Mrs. Worthington said.

"Nana, nana," Leo shouted as he ran towards his grandmother and climbed on her lap.

"What is it you wanted to talk about, Mrs. Worthington; I mean, Sonia?" Olive took a seat.

"Oh, nothing so important, Dear. Tell me how

are you doing, have you settled well? Are things getting easier?"

Olive studied Sonia and wondered how Blake could be her son considering how nice and polite she was. *I rarely see a glimpse of her in him, I know that deep down he is nice too, but I can't comprehend why he is so rude and aggressive towards me,* Olive thought.

"I'm fine, Sonia. Thank you for asking, it is really nice of you, but I'm fine nothing wrong. I like it here."

"I just called in to apologize, my Dear," Sonia said.

"Apologize for what?"

"I know it's already very tough for you to come here and work for a man who is ungrateful. I've heard the way he speaks to you. I'm afraid what happened with his wife was very hard on him. I doubt he will ever recover."

Olive nodded knowing it would be hard to lose a loved one. Her *grossmammi* and *grossdaddi* were still alive, but she knew that one day she would lose someone close.

Sonia continued, "Please forgive him; he's become aggressive towards everyone. I've given it some thought; I think he gets upset when he sees you taking care of Leo so well. It reminds him of her, and he lashes out in frustration."

"That makes sense. I appreciate you telling me this, Sonia. I thought that he scolded me because I wasn't doing my job properly, seeing as I've got no experience or training."

Sonia leaned forward and said, "I'm afraid you aren't in a winning position. No matter how well you look after Leo, Blake will most likely never be happy. It'll just remind him of how he lost Mona, his wife. He'll most likely come around in time, but please don't leave over his bad moods; Leo needs you."

"Thank you, that makes things easier for me. My mother told me to look at the other person's point of view. There are two sides to everything and we only know our side."

"Your mother is a wise woman."

Olive would not normally ask questions, but since Sonia offered her information she was curious to know more. "Did his wife die a long time ago?"

"Just about a year ago."

"Oh. And he's not met another woman since? I mean he is rich and handsome." Olive knew that comfort and wealth were important to *Englischers,* as well as the outer beauty of a person.

"Look here, sounds like you have a crush on my son?" Sonia raised an eyebrow.

Olive put her hand to her mouth as she giggled. "It's nothing like that. I mean, anyone would find him attractive; I was just making an observation." Sonia continued to look at her, which caused Olive to add, "He wouldn't suit me since he's not an Amish boy."

Sonia tossed her head back and laughed.

Olive felt heat rise in her cheeks. Sonia hadn't been serious and here she was explaining herself. Sonia would know she could not consider having anything to do with an *Englischer.* "I feel silly. I have a habit of blurting things out."

"Come on now, Olive, don't try to fool an old lady. I'm much older than I look. My natural hair color is white and thanks to a product known as Botox, my wrinkles are kept at bay. I didn't get to be this age without learning a thing or two about love." Sonia shook her head. "All women fall in love with my son, and the annoying thing is that he knows it. He could have any woman he wants; I'm sure of it." Sonia stared at Olive and said, "He'd do well to find a nice woman like you; that's just what he needs."

"No, it's not like that really. He was a little nice on the first day and from then on he's not been nice. Oh, I'm not complaining, just trying to point out that I couldn't possibly have a crush on someone like him."

"That simply won't do. I'll have a talk to him. He's got no right to be rude to you after you were so good to come here and work for us."

Olive put her hand to her mouth. "Please don't do that. Things will work themselves out I'm sure. If you were right about him being upset about his wife he needs to work things out in his own time."

"Very well, but if it continues for much longer you must let me know."

"I will," Olive said. "It's only natural that Blake would take a long time to get over his wife's death."

"Life can throw some strange things our way, but we have to keep moving."

Olive nodded thinking of the Scripture that the rain falls on the just and the unjust alike. Bad things can even happen to good people.

"Just remember, Dear, let me know if you need anything. You already take such good care of Leo. I'm sure you will eventually smooth things out with Blake too." Sonia patted Olive's hand. "I've some errands to run today. I'll call by again this afternoon and spend some time with Leo."

"Yes, Leo would love that." Olive and Leo said goodbye to Sonia and closed the door. *Blake must have some good in him since his mother is so lovely,* Olive thought as she walked up the stairs with Leo, *I must not think poorly of him.*

Chapter 7

Every good gift and every perfect gift is from above,
and cometh down from the Father of lights,
with whom is no variableness, neither shadow of
turning.
James 1:15

Driving like a reckless teenager, putting one hand on the horn and increasing speed, Blake remembered what happened at the breakfast table. He had told Olive many times not to feed Leo berries, and she did not remember one word of what he said. Why did she have trouble remembering that sometimes berries made Leo break out into a rash? A properly trained and qualified nanny would have a way of remembering something as important as allergies. He couldn't have her endangering her son's health, no matter how attractive and pleasant she was.

She just goes along and thinks that she can do as she pleases just because she's the only one who can make Leo do as she says. She has to learn that things have consequences. Maybe she doesn't realize the importance of her position as Leo's nanny.

Mother doesn't understand what kind of people there are in this world. Just because Olive's Amish doesn't mean that she's perfect. I need to find someone who can look after Leo properly, Blake thought. *Despite what my mother thinks, a mere girl can't be expected to take on the responsibility of Leo for any length of time. I never could understand my mother and how she thinks.*

Switching into fifth gear, Blake crossed 120 km/hr. without knowing that he had just exceeded the speed limit. Blake's already bad mood was not helped when the lights of a police car flashed in his rear view mirror.

After a brief exchange with the police officer, he produced his driver's license and was issued a ticket. The speeding ticket did nothing to help Blake's mood.

"This could be a sign that I have to do something about that woman. Enough is enough; I need to talk to mom. Maybe she can find Olive a job somewhere with one of her friends. I know Mom will have every excuse under the sun to keep Olive on, but it makes no sense. Leo needs to have a proper nanny look after him. It's not as if I can't afford it

* * *

Later that day, Sonia came back to the house to see Leo as promised. Sonia played with Leo in his playroom while Olive cleaned up.

"I'll wash some of Leo's clothes; his laundry basket is full." Olive carried the basket downstairs and into the laundry. She'd already noticed that there was a large electric washer and clothes dryer in there and she was keen to try it out. At her *haus* she had no clothes dryer at all and in the wet whether they hung their clothes on a line in the barn. Their washing machine was gas-powered and nowhere near the size of the one in Blake's house. It seemed strange to Olive that she could do the washing at any time of day and not just in the morning.

"Do you need any help, Olive?" Sonia called out, "I told you that we have people to clean once a week and that includes the weekly washing."

"No, I'm almost done in the laundry."

"Then when you're done can you give Leo a bath? He's just drawn all over himself with crayons and Blake will be furious if he sees him like that."

"I'll be right there." Olive hurried upstairs and gave Leo his bath. Once she had him dry and dressed in his pajamas, Olive heard a key clicking in the front door downstairs.

Sonia, who had joined them in Leo's bedroom, said, "That must be Blake."

Olive glanced across at Sonia, and they shared a knowing look. Olive knew that Sonia guessed she was nervous around him.

Leo heard his father downstairs. "Daddy, daddy." He bolted to the top of the stairs.

Olive held his hand and helped him down; Sonia followed along behind them.

When Blake scooped up Leo into his arms, Sonia

asked, "Blake, how was your day?"

"Not good. Amongst other things, I got a ticket for speeding."

"Oh, that's a bad day. Be careful when you drive next time," his mother said.

Blake frowned at his mother and sat down. "Can you please get me a glass of water, Olive?"

"Sure." Olive opened a bottle of cold water, poured it into a glass and went to walk back into the living room, but paused when she heard her name mentioned. Sonia and Blake were speaking about her.

"I want to talk to you about Olive," Blake said to his mother.

"Yes?" Sonia said.

"I don't know anything about this girl. She also isn't from our world; we know nothing about her except the few things she's told us. How can we hire some stranger to look after my son?"

"I'm confident that she's the right person for the job. Qualifications aren't everything. You just need to think positive. In fact, you need to be more positive in general. You're always looking at the worst side of things. She's been here for some time and she's doing splendidly."

Their conversation ended when Olive came back into the room with the water. "Blake, would you like to make you some dinner, or have you eaten out again?"

"I could do with a sandwich. That's all I feel like."

Olive nodded. "I'll fix you one." She hurried back into the kitchen and wondered if they would speak about her some more. She stayed by the entrance of the kitchen just in case they did.

"Leo is happy with her and she's treating him as her own son," Sonia said.

They had a few more things to say about her Olive was certain, but decided not to listen. Whatever Blake thought of her was something she could do nothing about. *If Gott wants me to work here then things will work out, and if not, then Gott will place me somewhere else,* Olive thought.

* * *

Olive was determined to do her best for Blake, but the man was making her crazy. He seemed to be searching for something, anything to point out as wrong. It had been three days since she'd overheard Blake reprimanding his mother for hiring her.

Taking a risk, Olive informed Blake that she thought it best that he eat dinner with his son every night. Blake pressed his lips together and gave a nod, which Olive took as a positive sign. She knew it was a good habit for the family to eat dinner together.

She had made it a point to arrive early that morning. Blake watched Leo draw on a large pad on the kitchen table. They both turned to look at her when she walked in.

There was a pile of clothes, and it appeared Blake had attempted to dress his son at some point. Blake didn't bat an eye as he pushed the small pile of clothes toward Olive. "I give up; you dress him." He continued to sip at his coffee.

Olive had no trouble in dressing Leo and not

long after that Blake left for work.

She cleaned up the breakfast dishes and searched the kitchen for a list, but there was none. "Well, I don't believe it!" Olive stood in the middle of the kitchen shocked that Blake had conceded a tiny bit of control. *No list of dos and don'ts.*

Leo often wore more food than he ate. Olive took him upstairs and changed his clothes once more. Once back in the living room they settled into a serious block building competition when someone came in through the front door. Olive quickly shielded Leo until she could figure out who it was.

She let out a relieved breath when it was just Blake's mother. "Hello, my lovely," she said to Leo. When she across at Olive, she said, "I was hoping to find you two at home."

"Nana, Nana!" Leo yelled and clapped in glee as he struggled to get out of Olive's hold.

Olive set him on the ground and watched the toddler leap into his grandmother's arms. Olive watched their interaction and left them alone.

The beautifully clothed and groomed woman

followed Olive into the kitchen and sat down watching Olive carefully. "So my dear, how are you doing with my boys?" The smile on her face was mischievous, yet she was serene at the same time.

Olive tried to laugh but faltered. "I think that I'm doing okay. I don't think Blake is happy with me, but we're still getting to know each other." She giggled to cover her nerves.

Sonia watched her a bit longer then rose to her feet. "Good, I think that we should get to know each other better too. I have an idea for the afternoon." She clapped her hands happy with her own idea. "There is a cartoon character ice show at the arena this week; I think we should treat our boy to a fun afternoon. Let's go, we have fun awaiting us." Sonia's enthusiasm was contagious, and soon Olive was preparing snacks and a drink for Leo.

They piled into Sonia's luxury sedan and headed off for a day full of surprises. Olive was curious and nervous about what the day would reveal, but she genuinely did like Blake's mother.

When they arrived at the show, Olive said, "Sonia, I won't go in. I'll stay in the car."

"You can't go in?"

Olive shrugged. "Most likely not."

"I understand. I think the show goes for an hour or more. Will you be alright here in the car?"

"*Jah*, of course. I'll just wait here. I'm happy to do that."

Olive sat and watched the little boy pull hard on Sonia's arm eager to get to his destination. Over an hour later they returned. Sonia looked exhausted, and even Leo looked tired. Olive strapped Leo in his seat and wrapped a blanket around him to fight off the chill.

"How was the show, Sonia?"

"The show went on and the kids in the arena cheered and laughed. Leo had so much fun." Sonia leaned in and whispered to Olive, "He's so much like his father you know. They are so happy and full of life." At Olive's disbelieving look, she laughed and continued, "No, I'm being serious. Blake was so full of life, so excited, but that all ended with the

Mona situation."

Olive knew that heartache could change a person. "Will you tell me what happened? I don't want to pry, but he seems so angry now. It can't be good for a person to hold all that anger inside."

Sonia's eyes watered as she nodded her head. She stared off into the car park and turned on the ignition. "They were high school sweethearts. Blake spent years building a name for himself in the business world before he proposed, and then a second later, they were pregnant."

Sonia's car joined the queue leaving the car park. Olive wondered whether Sonia missed Leo's mother.

"Mona was demanding and impossible throughout the pregnancy. She did not understand that Blake had to work to pay for her ever increasing, expensive lifestyle."

That's all Sonia said, and Olive did not want to pry further about the matter.

"Are you able to eat lunch with us at a bistro?" Sonia asked.

"Yes, I eat out often. My friends and I go to the same coffee shop nearly every week." Olive missed her friends; she had little of them lately.

Sonia drove to a bistro, and they found a table out in the garden. The women ordered their lunch and enjoyed Leo's silliness as he raced around after the birds.

The afternoon would have been perfect except Olive could not stop thinking about Blake and Mona. He had lost so much, no wonder he was angry all the time. Olive tried to imagine a happy and carefree version of Blake. The only version of him she could envision was the uptight, grumpy businessman who greeted her every day.

Leo was exhausted from his day and on the drive back to the house, he fell asleep in his car seat.

Once Sonia left, Olive cooked the dinner. With Leo still asleep, she could concentrate on cooking; it settled her mind.

Chapter 8

For the sun is no sooner risen with a burning heat,
but it withereth the grass, and the flower
thereof falleth,
and the grace of the fashion of it perisheth:
so also shall the rich man fade away in his ways.
James 1:11

After the last two weeks she'd had, Olive needed time with her four close friends. She organized them to meet at their favorite coffee shop on Saturday morning.

Olive was pleased when her older *bruder,* Elijah, offered to drive her into town and come fetch her two hours later. Her legs ached from the constant bike riding over the past weeks to and from Blake and Leo's house.

When Elijah asked her about her new job, she told him that she enjoyed it and loved looking after the little boy. She didn't tell him about her employer's bad moods and how she felt as though nothing she did was good enough.

The drive to the coffee shop was just enough time for her to plan what she would tell her friends. Olive knew from experience that her friends would be relentless in asking her questions to extract every detail of her new job.

The girls sat at their regular table. Soon tall steaming cups littered the table along with a variety of pastries. Often, they would each order a different pastry or cake and each girl would try a little of each.

"For someone who's just landed a well-paid job as a nanny you don't look very happy," Jessie's eyes bored through Olive's thin disguise of a smile.

Of all Olive's friends, she knew that Jessie would be the one to notice that something was not right.

Jessie watched her from across the table waiting for Olive to speak, but Amy spoke before her. "*Nee*, you don't look happy, Olive."

The girls all leaned in, waiting for her response.

She was tempted to shrug off their concerns and tell them everything was fine, but they knew her too well to do that. "Some things about the job are great. I love looking after Leo. The house is amazing, and Leo's grandmother is extremely nice."

"Then what's the problem?" one of the girls asked.

"Leo's father is grumpy with me all the time. I'm trying not to take it personally."

"Why's he grumpy?" Claire asked.

"Mrs. Worthington told me her son is angry all the time because he's deeply hurt." Olive lowered her voice. "His wife died about a year ago, and now it seems that he's cranky with the whole world, but he's just taking it out on me."

Her friends exchanged looks but said nothing. "You don't understand; his mother says that he was different before that. She said he was full of life and so much fun. Now, he's not happy about anything and he's taking it out on me."

"Why would he take it out on you?" Jessie asked.

"That day at the farmers' market Blake's mother gave me the job straight away. I guess Blake is mad with his mother for doing that and he can't take it out on her." Olive shrugged.

Claire leaned forward and held Olive's hand. "Um, Olive, can I ask you a question? What does Blake look like?" The other girls turned to her and waited for her to answer.

Olive thought about it and felt that the truth would not hurt. "He's attractive in an older-man sort of way. I can see how women might find him interesting. His mother, Sonia, says all women fall in love with him, and he could have any woman he wants." Olive pulled her hand away from Claire's.

Claire leaned back into her seat and slapped a hand over her mouth, stifling laughter that appeared to be bubbling. Amy playfully slapped Claire's arm and tried to remain serious.

It was the forthright Jessie who said, "So you think he's handsome, and you absolutely love his son; that's interesting."

Olive couldn't believe what she heard. That's not what she felt; he was just her employer and she had no other feelings for him except empathy for his situation.

Amy interrupted Olive's thoughts just in time. "We get it, Olive, I mean, it's not hard to fall in love with someone, but be careful. It's not fun to be delusional, but feel free to come to any of us if you need someone to talk to."

They all dissolved into laughter at the way Amy spoke, and Olive laughed with them. When they were through with laughing, they told Olive about each of their job situations.

The stall at the farmers' market had been successful for most of them. Jessie Miller found a position as a housekeeper and Amy Yoder obtained a position looking after an *Englicsh* lady's children after school, Saturdays and was 'on call' in emergencies. Amy was employed from the coming Monday, and Jessie Miller started her job in two weeks time. Claire Shonberger and Lucy Fuller had interviews to attend and were hopeful.

"Don't look so distressed, Olive, I was just teasing with what I said to you before about being in love with your boss. It was silly of me."

Olive smiled at Jessie's flashing, green eyes and said, "I know, I'm just a little concerned that one day he will tell me that I don't have a job anymore and I won't see Leo again. I'm trying not to worry because I know that won't help anything. I keep telling myself if *Gott* wants me there then He will have me stay and if *Gott* wants me somewhere else, then He will put me somewhere else."

"You're right as usual. You were right for us to all advertize ourselves on the stall the other week. We're all going to get jobs out of it, it seems," Jessie said.

"*Jah denke,* Olive," Amy said.

The other girls chimed in with thanking Olive, but were cut short when Dan placed a plate of chocolate fudge in the centre of their table. "You girls can be taste-testers and tell me what you think of our new chocolate fudge slice."

Olive was sure that the five of them were his favorite customers because he always showed them special attention. As always, he had a special smile for Lucy, which made her blush.

That night, Olive made sure she helped her *mudder* cook the dinner since she was not there to help her of a weeknight. Their conversation quickly turned to Blake. "He's cranky with me all the time, *Mamm*. His *mudder,* Sonia, said it's because his wife died a year ago and he's upset with the world. It didn't help things that his *mudder* employed me without consulting him."

"*Jah*, that wouldn't help him. *Menner* like to feel as though they're in charge."

Olive carefully shelled the peas while she listened to the wisdom of her *mudder.* "If someone is mean to you or rude and you remain polite, then that person will see that you aren't matching their ways."

"And?" Olive asked after her *mudder* left out the part about how that would help the situation.

With a laugh her *mudder* added, "He will see how rude he's been and might correct his manners himself."

"That makes sense; then I just pay his temper no mind?"

"*Jah*, that's right. Just be sure that working for an *Englischer* is not going to lead you into the ways of the world."

"*Jah*, I know. *Dat* has already mentioned that to me."

"We miss having you around the *haus*, but I suppose it had to happen some day. I hoped it would be for a different reason."

"*Mamm*, there are no *menner* around for me. None of my friends have boys interested in them either. Seems in our community there are many more girls than *menner*. That's why this job is a good idea. In the future, I might be able to buy myself a little *haus,* or at least afford a lease on one."

"Olive, I don't like hearing you speak of such things. Trust the *gut* Lord to bring you a *mann.*"

Olive turned to her sweet *mudder* and smiled. "I will, *Mamm*." She hoped she would meet a *gut mann* someday, so her *mudder* and *vadder* would be happy. But, Olive did not see how it could possibly happen for her.

Chapter 9

Blessed is the man that endureth temptation:
for when he is tried, he shall receive the crown of life,
which the Lord hath promised to them that love him.
James 1:12

Since it was raining heavily, Olive had one of her *bruders* drive her to Blake's house. She'd have to think up indoor things that she and Leo could do today. They normally played in the park or the yard, but now, with the approaching cold weather she would have to think up new games.

That morning, Blake seemed calmer, which was a surprising change. Leo had loved the pancakes she'd made and even Blake had stolen a couple before he left. She didn't say a word about it but had smiled secretly.

Even after talking it through with her friends recently, Olive still could not get Blake's late wife out of her mind. As she wandered around the house, she realized that there were no pictures of his wife anywhere. She knew for a fact that *Englischers* often displayed photographs in their homes.

Without even thinking about it, her feet shuffled from room to room. Every time she entered a new space, Olive searched for any sign of his wife, but there was none to be found. She knew there was nothing in Leo's bedroom. She had never seen one picture or keepsake anywhere in the whole house. Olive decided that Blake must have loved her so much that he could not bear any reminder of her anywhere at all.

Leo would never remember his mother because of his age, so it would be up to his family to tell him about her. Olive could not imagine not having her mother around when she was growing up.

How would Leo ever learn what his mother was like? Would Blake speak of her or would his heartache prevent him from sharing memories with Leo? She knew it was none of her business, and they were *Englischers,* so most likely did things in a very different manner.

Olive finished the small amount of chores that

she'd taken on before Leo woke from his nap. He was so full of energy that Olive was irritated by the weather that kept them trapped indoors. She remembered an old game her *mudder* had used when she and her brothers couldn't go outside because of either the rain or the snow. Olive gathered a few sheets from the linen cupboard and went to work. Leo was excited about all the building she was doing and happily helped her. After they gathered some snacks from the kitchen, they climbed into their new tent.

Olive had moved the furniture to allow her to create the large tent-like structure. She pulled in some of Leo' toys and books. Together they enjoyed eating their snacks and playing with Leo's toys.

The sound of Leo's laughter was becoming her favorite sound. Olive didn't think she laughed as much with the girls as she did with two-year-old Leo. From blocks, they moved on to reading a couple of stories. Leo loved the different voices she made for the characters and sat through two whole stories before his attention evaporated.

The rain outside was coming down in sheets, but in their make-shift tent Olive and Leo couldn't have cared less.

Olive looked at the clock. Blake would soon be home. "Come on, Leo, we have to clean up. Daddy will be home soon. You can help me with the dinner."

Even though Blake seemed no less angry, Olive had got him to agree to come home earlier every night to eat dinner with Leo. In a quiet moment, Blake had confessed that he hardly saw his own father because he constantly worked. Maybe *Gott* had put her in that family to make a difference in their lives.

During dinner that night, Blake said, "Tell me about being Amish, Olive."

It was a rare, quiet moment in which Leo was occupied trying to stab a pea with his fork.

"I don't know any other way of living." She looked up at Blake and realized that she had given him an insufficient answer. "What exactly would you like to know?"

"What are your thoughts on God? When I was younger, I went to church, searching for the meaning of life, but I never found it. I often wonder why we're all here."

"We're all here to live our lives for God. We won't be here for long; our real home is with God."

"What is the purpose of us being here; why aren't we with God now if that's what He wants?"

"I guess He wants to find the faithful ones."

Blake looked down at his chicken and carefully cut a piece. "I was searching and then I couldn't find any answers. I guess I buried myself in my work."

"The difference with us is that we don't live for this life, but for the one we have with God."

"Hmm, I see that."

"We never know how long God will give us on this earth before He calls us home." As soon as she said it she wished she hadn't. Speaking of death would only remind him of Mona. She looked across at him, but he was busily eating as if he wasn't worried by what she said.

Their peace was shattered when Leo saw how far he could throw the peas.

Chapter 10

Wherefore, my beloved brethren, let every
man be swift to hear,
slow to speak, slow to wrath:
For the wrath of man worketh not the
righteousness of God.
James 1:19-20

The next Friday when Olive came to work, Blake surprised her by announcing he was not going to work that day.

Olive's jaw dropped, and for a moment she was lost for words. "The whole day?" she eventually asked.

He nodded. It was a perfect seventy-degree day, not a cloud in the sky.

"Do you want me to go home since you will be here?" Olive offered looking down at Leo's excited face.

"No, I'd like you to come with us. We're going to find a nice spot and go for a swim in one of the creeks before the cold sets in."

"Might be a little late for that; the sun's out, but it's not that warm."

"It's only early in the day; it'll warm up. You're always telling me that I should spend more time with him." Blake glanced at Olive briefly. "I guess his mother always did this stuff with him," he muttered. "I know you're right about me spending time with Leo since I hardly got to know my father. Perhaps you can pack us one of those picnics you used to have as a child?"

Olive smiled. "I didn't think you were listening the other morning."

"The key to my success is to listen to the advice of others. Providing that the people who are giving the advice know what they are talking about."

"That's a compliment, is it? You're saying that I know what I'm talking about when I speak about my childhood?"

"You're good with Leo; that has to come from your own upbringing since you've no formal training."

Olive was quick to change the subject from her lack of training. "I'll pack us a *wunderbaar* picnic."

Blake chuckled.

"Before that, would you like coffee?" Olive asked.

"Absolutely." Blake sat on a kitchen stool. "Should we stop by your home, so you can get your bathers?"

Olive swung her head around toward him. "No, I can't wear them. I mean Amish don't wear them -ever."

"What do you swim in?"

She looked down at her clothes. "Just our clothes."

"Seems as though that would be dreadfully uncomfortable."

Olive shrugged and put the cup under the outlet of the built-in coffee machine. "I don't know anything else." She turned back toward him once the coffee cup was filled to the brim. "The Amish consider it not modest to show too much skin."

"Ah," he said as he nodded thanks for his coffee.

Feeling uneasy, Olive said, "I won't go into the water today. I only ever went for a swim on the hottest days."

"Daddy, come *wit'* us?" Leo asked his father in the broken words of a toddler.

Olive answered, "Yes, daddy's coming with us today, and we're going to have a picnic. Just like we had in the tent the other day."

Olive could barely contain her smile at the thought of Blake spending time with his son. Maybe Blake's barriers were breaking down.

"Let me make a few phone calls while you load him into his car seat."

Leo squealed in excitement knowing that they were all going out in the car.

Olive and Leo waited in the car for a long time while Blake made phone calls. Leo tried to peel the seatbelt off his shoulders. Just as Olive had given up on Blake and was opening the door to pull Leo out of the car, he climbed into the driver's seat.

"Everybody ready?" Blake turned the key in the ignition while Olive shut the car door.

"I've heard that the *Englisch* have play groups where they can interact with other children," Olive said.

Blake glanced at Olive. "I suppose my mother mentioned that?"

Olive nodded.

"You can enroll him if you wish," Blake said.

"It's just that I notice that he keeps to himself even when we go to the park with other children. He doesn't speak to them."

Blake raised his eyebrows, which caused Olive to add, "I'm used to children playing well together and I notice that Leo likes to be by himself. Your mother mentioned something about it too."

"Sure, good idea."

Olive frowned at Blake. Was he listening to her at all?

After a silent period Blake said, "Good idea to enroll him in a children's group."

Olive had run out of things to say and Blake wasn't saying anything. She did not know how she felt about spending the day with her boss. She was particularly embarrassed at him thinking she was odd for swimming in her clothes. But what could she expect of an *Englischer*? It would be perfectly understandable and acceptable to an Amish man.

Blake was attractive she had to admit, but a wealthy and successful man like Blake would not even consider her as a suitable match even if she were *Englisch*. Men like him weren't likely to be attracted to a nanny, much less an Amish nanny who swam in clothing and closed her eyes to thank *Gott* before every meal. She wondered what the two of them would have in common or talk about if they were a couple. Their worlds were so different from one another.

The more she thought about Blake, the faster Olive's heart beat. Blake, in contrast, seemed comfortable and quiet in the driver's seat, intently listening to a business radio show pouring through the speakers. His lack of small talk in the car made Olive unusually uncomfortable.

"Yay! We here!" Leo shouted with glee, once the car stopped.

Olive was relieved that the tension in the car had broken. Before Olive could open her door, Leo had nearly peeled himself from his five-point harness. Olive pulled Leo from his car seat, while trying to balance the picnic basket and tote bag on her other arm. Blake must have noticed because he took Leo from her arms.

Blake and Leo chose a grassy spot on the bank in which to spread out the picnic blanket. The area they chose was not too close to the water, but still had some pleasant shade from an old oak tree. Olive giggled when she saw Blake's fancy business shoes with traces of sand beading up on them. "You should change. I mean your shoes."

"I guess I should." Blake stood up, walked a little distance, took off his shoes and socks and rolled up his trousers slightly. When he came closer, he said, "I was going to go for a swim, but since it doesn't appear you will go in, then neither will I."

Olive smiled with relief. She did not know what she would do if she saw him half dressed.

"So what kind of things did Leo's mom do with

him?" she asked trying to understand their situation better and learn something of Mona.

Blake looked away from her and shrugged. "The usual things."

"Leo needs to spend time with you. Maybe you can do something with him again tomorrow, but by yourselves."

"I'm going to be busy tomorrow. Besides, I hire you to take care of Leo's needs."

Olive guessed that Blake would have his mother watch Leo tomorrow since it would be Saturday and she was only employed Monday through Friday. Maybe, he had to work tomorrow to make up for having today off.

The two of them sat in silence for a time and watched Leo run around. To get away from Blake Olive took Leo into the water's edge to splash around. Her head hurt from trying to think of nice things to say to Blake, so she put him out of her mind and enjoyed playing with Leo.

Things did not improve while they ate. Olive considered it best to ignore Blake and not make any attempt to speak to him. Whatever she said was the wrong thing, it seemed.

"We should have gotten something to eat somewhere," Blake muttered under his breath.

"Sandwiches not good enough for you? It is a picnic and there wasn't much in the fridge today."

He scratched his head. "I'm trying to stay away from gluten."

He could have told me that before I made the sandwiches, Olive thought. "How about we stop for ice-cream on the way home?"

"Very well," Blake agreed in a monotone voice.

It was no surprise to Olive that their trip to the ice-cream shop was much the same as their picnic had been. As they sat at a table in the ice-creamery, Blake occasionally corrected Leo about something and ignored Olive completely. The rest of the time, Blake checked either his cell phone or his watch, as if he had somewhere more important to be.

The drive home was filled with even more painful and awkward silence. Leo fell asleep in the back seat, the result of hours of fresh air and a belly full of ice cream. The boring business pod-cast droned over the car's speakers, nearly lulling Olive to sleep.

Olive had a lot of time to think while she was in the car. She was tired from the day and grateful that it was nearly over. If it weren't for sweet little Leo, she would surely turn down this job and Blake's money. Like her mother always said, some things just aren't worth the headache.

Chapter 11

Ye are my witnesses, saith the Lord,
and my servant whom I have chosen:
that ye may know and believe me, and understand
that I am he:
before me there was no God formed, neither shall
there be after me.
Isaiah 43:10

It wasn't even dinnertime when they got home from their day out, but Leo was fast asleep. While Olive unpacked everything they took with them, Blake carried Leo to bed.

When Olive came inside, she heard Blake's cell phone beep and he went into his den and came out ten minutes later.

Olive looked up to see a much happier Blake come into the kitchen.

"Good news?" she asked.

"Yes, that phone call was about a deal that I've just pulled off. I've been worried about it all day.

A company was going to sign one of our contracts and balked at the last minute, but they've just signed it." Blake heaved a sigh.

She knew nothing of his business and nor did she desire to know if it affected his moods so. "Leo didn't wake up when you put him down?"

Blake shook his head and smiled. "He's fast asleep."

Blake sat down in the kitchen instead of making phone calls in his den. "Are you happy here, Olive?"

"Yes, I love it here." She studied his face and noticed he looked serious. Olive hoped that he would not say he had no more need for her services. "Would you like some coffee?"

He nodded. "Please. I was shocked when you first came here when I saw that you were Amish. My mother told me how good you were with Leo, but she said nothing about you being Amish." He cleared his throat then added, "I wouldn't have thought you could take a job such as this. I thought you Amish kept to yourselves."

"Many people work outside the community. We don't socialize with *Englischers* though."

Blake chuckled.

Olive spun around from scooping the coffee into the stainless steel compartment of the coffee maker. "What's so funny?"

"I'm sorry, it just sounds funny to call people who aren't Amish *Englischers*. I have heard it before though. It's a funny word; I wonder where it came from."

Olive shrugged her shoulders; she knew, but was too tired to tell him. *He seems to be talking now that he's at home,* Olive thought. *Strange that he did not want to speak when we were out.*

"Tell me something about your family, Olive. You know more about me than I know about you."

"I'm the middle child. I have three older sisters, one young sister and two younger brothers."

"That's quite a crew."

"We had a lot of fun together growing up, playing with all the animals. Mind you, it wasn't all fun; we had a lot of chores to do as well. As soon as we could walk we had to do chores, but when we did them together it wasn't so bad."

"Did your parents have a working farm?"

Olive nodded. "Still do. My father has a dairy farm, and we children raised pigs and chickens. There were so many animals around when we were growing up."

"Since Leo has no brother or sisters and isn't likely to ever have any, I've been thinking of getting him a pet, maybe a dog. But, I'll wait until he's older."

Olive felt sad for Blake that he had so many years ahead of him and never wanted to get married again. He must have loved his wife so much that he could not contemplate the thought of loving another. "That would be a wonderful idea. He'd love to have a dog to take care of. It'll teach him responsibility and he'll have someone to care for. But I will look into that play group idea."

"Well, Olive, it sounds like you had the ideal childhood; no wonder you're so good with Leo."

"Ah, you think I'm good with Leo?"

Blake threw back his head and laughed, but he did not answer her.

"You really think I'm good with Leo?" Olive asked once more; she had to know.

"Of course, he adores you."

Olive smiled and knew that he was satisfied that he could trust her to look after his young son.

"Does that surprise you?" Blake asked.

Olive laughed a little. "You weren't too happy about me coming to work for you to begin with, were you?"

Blake smiled. "I was a little apprehensive since you had no experience."

"Your mother was insistent that I would be good for the job. I told her that I had no experience and told her about my friend, Amy; she's the one who's got the experience with children. Your mother didn't want to know about anyone else."

"I suppose mother might know best after all." Blake chuckled. "I'm sorry I gave you such a hard time when you first arrived here. I guess I was being protective of Leo. It was all too sudden since my mother insisted she be the only one to look after Leo. I wasn't expecting her to go out shopping one day and hire a nanny."

"Mothers can be like that sometimes." Olive stared at the floor while she thought of her *mudder* who did things her own way. The coffee machine churned signaling that the coffee was ready. She pressed the button for his black coffee then placed the mug in front of him.

"Thanks." He nodded and took a sip. When he placed the mug back down on the table, he said, "You might as well finish early today, Olive. Leo won't wake up 'til much later."

"Are you sure? I could fix you some dinner." It was a couple of hours before the time he usually came home.

"No, you deserve a little time off. I'd drive you home if Leo weren't asleep."

"I don't mind riding the bike; it's kind of peaceful."

Olive pulled her coat up around her neck and set off toward home. When she was a little way up the road, her mind kept drifting toward Blake. *Sometimes I catch him looking at me differently, has done so for days. I think he might like me. Nee, he couldn't possibly like me. He's probably happy that he knows that I'm gut for looking after Leo. A man like him would have a fancy Englischer wife, someone like his mudder, but younger.*

Chapter 12

I have not hid thy righteousness within my heart;
I have declared thy faithfulness and thy salvation:
I have not concealed thy lovingkindness
and thy truth from the great congregation.
Psalm 40:10

The next Monday, Olive arrived at Blake's house to find Sonia there on a visit. In the early days, Sonia had called in nearly every day to check on her, but now her visits were less frequent.

Leo rushed toward Olive when Sonia opened the door; a few minutes later he settled down and played with some blocks in the living room.

When Olive noticed that Blake was not frantically rushing about, she asked Sonia, "Has Blake left already."

"Yes, he left about five minutes ago. It's so much quieter without him, isn't it?"

Olive knew at that moment she was in trouble. She had a crush on her boss otherwise she would not have been so disappointed that she would not see him until the evening. "Yes, it is a lot quieter. Can I get you tea or coffee, Sonia?"

"Tea, please."

"Mum, mum," Leo muttered while he was playing.

"Leo, you must never say that." Leo looked up at Sonia with a look of confusion on his face.

Olive was about to head to the kitchen when she saw and heard their exchange. *Be quiet, Olive. It's none of your business,* she told herself. She was sure that Leo was just mumbling things. He didn't know anyone as Mum and could not have known what the word meant, so what was so terrible?

As she made the tea, Olive knew she had to find out more about Leo's mother. Should she dare to ask Sonia when she had such a reaction to Leo mentioning her?"

Why wouldn't Blake and his mother encourage Leo to talk about his mother? Something felt wrong.

When Blake's grandmother joined her in the

kitchen leaving Leo playing in the living room, Olive saw that as an opportunity to ask some questions.

It was Sonia who spoke first. "Olive, I saw the look on your face just now when I scolded Leo for saying mum."

Olive opened her mouth slightly, and then Sonia flung up her hand. "Don't even try to deny it; I can read you like a book." Sonia sat down at the kitchen table. "You see it would upset Blake to hear Leo mention the word."

"But don't you think that's a little unrealistic? Leo should be able to speak about his mother and should learn of the great love that his father and his mother once shared."

"Humph. Great love? Well, yes. I mean…" Sonia stammered, her kind eyes closing for a second.

Olive could tell that Sonia was upset by the topic of Leo's mother.

Sonia opened her eyes and said, "Heavens. I guess it won't hurt to tell you. There's not much to the story really. We don't share the details because we don't want Leo to be hurt when he gets older when he finds out the truth about his mother." Sonia leaned forward and spoke in a low voice so Leo wouldn't be able to hear. "I suppose it's time you found out. Blake's wife was killed when she was running off with Blake's good friend. They were driving off together, had the car accident, and she was killed instantly."

Olive gasped and held her stomach.

"The first Blake knew of things was two minutes after he arrived home one night and two police officers knocked on the door and gave him the news. He's never been the same. She ran off with no word. All her things were gone, money cleaned out of their joint account and everything. Her lover had been driving, and he was badly injured. I'm not sure what happened to him afterwards. Blake has never mentioned him to me and I'm not about to ask."

"Where was Leo at the time?"

"Mona brought him over to my house saying she had a doctor's appointment and would pick him up later that day." Sonia looked into the distance. "I thought she was overdressed to be going to the doctor."

"Thank you for telling me, Sonia. It all makes sense now. I mean Blake's anger."

Sonia nodded. "He's a broken man."

"I wondered why there was no sign of her anywhere in the house." Olive wondered what they would tell Leo about his mother when he got older. Would he ever learn what his mother was like, she must have had good qualities; would he ever learn of those? It was none of her business, Olive reminded herself.

"Why would anyone cheat on Blake? He had money, he was polished and successful, and the two of them had an amazing little boy together," Sonia said. "Left behind was a little note and her little boy. What kind of woman would choose another man over her own son?" She sighed. "I guess we should have seen it coming. Leo's mother was always so very needy of his attention."

"My mother always says that there are two sides

to everything."

Sonia scoffed. "What that woman did was unforgivable. Nothing in the world could justify what she did running away like that and leaving Leo."

"I can imagine how this has been hard on Blake, but even harder on Leo. A little boy needs his mother," Olive agreed as she poured the tea into Sonia's cup.

"I don't blame him for taking down those photos. What man wouldn't? They were just painful reminders of Mona's infidelity."

Olive finally understood what Blake and Leo had been through.

"There were photos up somewhere?" She was right about the photos.

"Yes, there were photos in the living room. I'll show you a photo of the three of them. They made such a beautiful family. I've got a photo in my handbag." Sonia trotted over to the other side of the kitchen and retrieved a small photo.

Olive took the photo and studied it. The woman

was fair and small, not unlike herself, yet this woman was most attractive. Blake looked years younger even though the photo was taken just over a year ago. "Leo had his curls even at that age." Olive smiled.

Sonia grabbed the photo back. "Mona looks a little like you."

"I suppose; we've both got fair hair and we're the same slight build."

"Hmm." Sonia tossed the photo on the kitchen bench beside her handbag.

Sonia didn't stay long after her cup of tea.

In the late afternoon, Olive noticed that the small photo was lying on the kitchen bench. Leo was drawing at his small table in the living room. She had to hide the photo somewhere until she could give it back to Sonia.

She does look a little like me, she thought again as she studied the photo.

"What have you got there?"

Olive clutched the photo and spun around. "Blake, I didn't hear you come in."

"I came in the front way. So what has you so interested?"

Frowning she placed the photo down on the bench. How would she explain this?

Blake's eyes fell to the photo and his face grew red. He bellowed, "What in tarnation are you doing with that?"

She could feel tears come to her eyes; no one had ever yelled at her like that. Her breathing grew heavy as she tried to talk herself out of crying. She could not speak.

"Well? Answer me."

Tears flowed down Olive's cheeks. She'd been holding it in for weeks; he'd been so horrible to her and she was ignoring it, as her *mudder* had told her. But now, it was too much. She covered her face with both her hands as tears flowed from her eyes.

"I'm so sorry," Blake said as he wrapped his warm arms around her.

She leaned into the hardness of his chest and cried some more. When her tears subsided, she stepped away from him. He reached for the box of tissues behind him and handed some to her.

"Your mother told me about your wife and showed me the photo. She left it here by mistake. I was only looking at it." Olive dabbed her eyes. "I was going to hide it somewhere so you wouldn't see it; so you wouldn't be upset."

Blake put his head down. "I'm a beast. Forgive me, Olive. I've upset you."

"Yes, you've upset me and you upset me most days." Olive sniffed some more and wiped her eyes.

"I've been intolerable. There's no excuse for my behavior. I should have told you about Leo's mother. It wasn't a secret; I suppose it's the reason for my ugly temper."

Leo ran into the room and looked at both of them. He hugged Olive around her knees, which caused Olive to smile.

"I'll drive you home, Olive. We can put your bike in the trunk."

Olive nodded and sniffed some more. "I'll just

go and splash some cold water on my face, so my family don't see I've been crying."

When they arrived at her parents' house, she glanced over at Blake to thank him for driving her. She noticed he was staring at her with a soft look in his eyes.

"Olive, would you come to dinner with me one night?"

Olive felt as though she could not breathe for an instant. She was attracted to him, but would he always be angry? Was she willing to compromise herself to go on a date with an *Englisch* man? "You mean like a date?"

"Exactly like a date because it will be a date," he answered, looking at her lips.

"I don't know."

He looked away from her. "I see."

"Blake, it isn't as simple as that. I can't go out to dinner with you you're not Amish."

He nodded, still not looking at her. "I see," he repeated, his voice almost a whisper.

Olive opened the door. "I'd better go. Someone's

sure to be watching us from the window."

Blake opened his door. "I'll get your bike out."

Olive turned to say goodbye to Leo, but saw that he was already asleep in the backseat. She met Blake at the back of the car.

"I always seem to be apologizing to you, Olive."

She shook her head. "There's no need." She reached out for the handlebars of the bike and in the dark she put her hand on his. She left her hand there and did not pull away.

He lightly touched her hand and whispered, "Don't give up on me, Olive."

He slid his hand away, and she grabbed the bike to steady it as he walked back to the car. She wheeled her bike toward the barn while she listened to the hum of his car drive away.

"Was that Blake?" Her older brother asked when she walked into the house.

Olive nodded. "He said it was too cold for me to ride my bike."

"I'll drive you and fetch you from now on," he said with a firm tone.

131

"*Denke*." Olive knew that her brother was not concerned with the cold he was concerned with her getting too close to her *Englisch* employer.

"You're early today," Olive's *mudder* said as she walked into the kitchen to help with the dinner.

"*Jah*, I am. Blake drove me home because it was too cold."

"You've ridden home on colder nights." Her *mudder* peered into her face. "Have you been crying?"

"Just a cold coming on, I think. That's why he drove me home." Normally Olive told her *mudder* everything, but tonight she did not have the energy to explain the whole situation to her.

Could Blake be in love with her? She had controlled her attraction toward him, but to find out that he felt the same would make things very difficult. How much longer could she contain her feelings and her attraction toward him?

Olive sighed. *If only he were Amish my world would be perfect. He would not be angry and we would get married and Leo would be my son too.*

She shook herself to rid herself of silly notions. Blake was not Amish and there was only once chance in a million that he would ever change his life and become Amish. *People do though, she told herself. I've seen five families become Amish in my lifetime. Jah, families, but not a single man with a child,* she realized. She remembered that Sonia told her that Blake had many women who had fallen in love with him. She was only one of many.

Chapter 13

But to him that worketh not,
but believeth on him that justifieth the ungodly,
his faith is counted for righteousness.
Romans 4:5

When Olive woke the next morning, Blake was still on her mind. How could she go back there when she had cried in his arms? Still in bed, she shut her eyes tightly and remembered the feel of being held in his strong arms, her head leaning into the hardness of his chest.

What had he meant when he said not to give up on him? Most likely he meant not to leave the job over his temper outbursts. *Jah, that's all it would be,* she thought wishing he had meant something regarding a future romance. *Don't be silly, Olive, he's a grown man, and he sees you as nothing more than a nanny. He would only have asked me out to dinner to make amends for his behavior. There are only so many times he can say he's sorry, and this is just another way to say it.*

Blake was right there to open the door for her when she knocked on it. She looked down to see Leo clasped around his father's ankles.

"Good morning, Leo."

"Good morning, Ollie."

Olive giggled as she usually did when Leo said her name. She was nervous to see Blake again, but his ready smile put her at ease.

"Since I've got an early start I'd better make a move. If I can, I'll be home early."

"That would be good, wouldn't it, Leo?" Olive bent down to Leo's height.

"Ya." He swung onto her neck freeing his father.

"I want to speak to you when I get home too," Blake said to Olive.

Olive smiled and nodded then Leo and she watched Blake as he walked out the door.

Throughout the day, Olive wished that Blake had not mentioned he wanted to speak to her about something; she could not stop worrying over what it might be. Did he want to end her employment?

All she could do was wait until he returned. That day the cleaner arrived at the same time as the food delivery. Once Olive put all the food away, she took Leo outside to play, so they would not get in the cleaners way.

When Blake returned home, he played with Leo for a while and then sat down on the couch with Olive. "I want to explain about Mona to you."

Olive blinked rapidly and looked away. "It's not necessary to say anything."

"Yes, it is. I was not a good husband to her. I left her alone with Leo and she got lonely. I was busy at work and even when I was here I was either on the laptop or the cell phone. It's my fault what she did; I hardly spoke to her. She would have been incredibly lonely."

Olive nodded.

Blake continued, "I've got deep regret over what I did. I wasn't a proper husband. All I wanted was a family. I took all of what I had for granted. I kept thinking we could have it all if only I worked a little harder or a little longer. Thinking in a few years, we could enjoy ourselves without me having to work so hard."

"Now is all we have," Olive said.

"I've realized that."

Olive squirmed in her seat. "I should get going; it's getting late."

"I'll drive you."

"*Nee,* my *bruder* is waiting for my call and then he'll come get me." Olive realized that in her nervousness she had just spoken a few words of Pennsylvania Dutch to an *Englischer.* She hoped that Elijah would be in the barn when her call came through, so she wouldn't have to wait at Blake's house any longer than necessary. He answered on the third ring. When Elijah told her that he already had the horse and buggy ready to leave, Olive heaved a sigh of relief and ended the call.

"I've disappointed you, haven't I?" Blake said.

"It's not for me to judge. Your personal life is none of my concern. I'm just Leo's nanny; I'm concerned for him, is all."

"I had hoped that you would like to be a little

138

more than that."

Olive shook her head. "Nothing could ever work between us. We're too different. The Amish have different levels of commitment to marriage than it appears other people do. I would never get married unless it was for life; it can be no other way."

"It seems that I'm always hurting the people I care for."

Olive was uneasy to hear him speak of his late wife and their unhappiness. "I'll wait outside for my brother."

"Olive, don't leave like this. I'm sorry if I've said too much."

"It's best I wait outside. My brother won't be far away."

Olive said goodbye to Leo and hurried down the driveway. The weather was colder, but Olive was too much amazed by what she had just leaned to take any notice. Her *familye* were right to be concerned about her working amongst the *Englisch.* She hoped that she hadn't put any of her friends in a similar situation with her silly idea that they should all become maids. Two of them had already gotten jobs with *Englischers.*

Olive wanted to share what she had learned about Blake, so she could have the benefit of someone else's opinion, but in whom could she confide? Her *mudder* would never let her go back there if she breathed a word of it and learned of her feelings for Blake. She could tell one of her friends and the one who would tell her what she really thought would be Jessie. She would see Jessie at the gathering on Sunday. No, it was too long to wait. Olive decided to go and visit Jessie, but she would have to wait until her next day off which would be Saturday.

Chapter 14

That if thou shalt confess with thy mouth
the Lord Jesus,
and shalt believe in thine heart that God hath
raised him from the dead, thou shalt be saved.
Romans 10:9

All was quiet when Olive arrived at Jessie's *haus* on the Saturday morning. She walked around to the back of the house and stuck her head through the back door. "Jessie."

"Olive? Is that you, Olive?

Olive stepped through the door. "*Jah*, it's Olive. Where are you?"

"I'm upstairs in my bedroom. Come up."

It appeared that Jessie's parents were out. Jessie's mother was always in the kitchen and of a Saturday Jessie's *daed* was usually reading on the couch in the living room. Olive made her way through the kitchen, the living room and walked up the wooden stairs.

She found Jessie in her room, dressed all but her prayer *kapp*.

"I'm running a little late today," Jessie said as she ran a brush through her wavy hair.

"Are you going somewhere?"

"*Nee*, I've nothing to do but some chores today."

"Oh, Jessie," Olive said as she flopped down on Jessie's bed.

Jessie rushed to sit next to her. "What is it? Job not going well?"

"I don't know where to begin. It's almost too awful to speak of."

"Tell me."

Olive looked into Jessie's intelligent green eyes and knew that of all people she would be the person she could talk to about the whole sorry thing.

After she told Jessie everything about her feelings for Blake, Jessie stared into the distance.

"Say something, Jessie. I thought you'd give me some advice – tell me to leave the job or something."

"It's not the first time that an Amish woman has

fallen in love with an *Englischer*."

Olive nodded. "Should I stay there?"

"You can't just change jobs because of something like that." Jessie looked deeply into Olive's eyes. "Unless, he feels the same way, does he?" Jessie raised her eyebrows.

Olive winced. "That's the trouble. He's as good as admitted that he likes me."

"*Ach.* That complicates things. Maybe you should leave. The bishop says we should not make a place for sin. The closer we go to the edge of the cliff the more likely we are to fall off – that's what the bishop said Sunday last."

Olive nibbled on her nails. "*Jah*, I remember." This was not what Olive wanted to hear. Why wasn't Jessie telling her it would be okay to stay? "Maybe if I pray about it things will turn out well."

Jessie screwed up her face. "You mean you want to marry him or something?"

"Don't be like that, Jessie. Some *Englischers* have joined the community."

"*Jah*, but more often it's the Amish who leaves

the community." When Olive did not respond, Jessie added, "Has he ever said anything about becoming Amish?"

"He's asked some questions."

"Well, what does he do for work? Could he still work if he joined us even if the bishop allowed him to join?"

Olive took a deep breath. "I'm not sure what he does. I think he does something at an office somewhere."

Jessie put her head in her hands. "Olive, you're not thinking straight. Just because there's no *menner* in the community for us doesn't mean you go out looking amongst the *Englischers*."

"*Nee*, Jessie. I wasn't doing that at all." Olive grabbed Jessie's hand. "Jessie, I had a thought on the way over here."

"What was that?" Jessie smiled.

"What about my *bruder* for you?"

"Which one?"

"Elijah. He's not married. What about him? He asked where I was going this morning and I noticed that he had a funny look on his face when I said that I was coming here to see you."

Jessie gave a little giggle. "Really? He never looks twice at me."

"Let me see what I can do." Olive thought that one of them amongst their group of friends should be married and her *bruder*, Elijah, was a fine *mann*.

"*Nee*, Olive, don't you say one thing to him. I'd be embarrassed."

"Better to be embarrassed once and then be married." Olive giggled. "You've got nothing to lose. I'll ask him what he thinks of you. Maybe he could take you on a buggy ride."

"Wasn't he courting Becca Miller?"

"A long time ago, but that didn't work out. Think about it, we could be *schweschders*."

When Olive left Jessie's *haus,* she felt no better. Maybe she wanted Jessie to say that she thought it was alright for her to stay working for Blake.

* * *

When Monday morning came, Olive felt as if it had been two months rather than two days since she had seen both Leo and Blake.

When she arrived at the door, it swung open, and Blake filled the doorway.

"Hello, Blake."

"I'm glad you came back. I was a little worried that you might not."

Olive said nothing as she walked inside. She looked around for Leo. "It's very quiet in here."

"My mother's got Leo."

Olive frowned.

"I need to talk to you, Olive. Let's sit in the living room."

This is where I get fired. I'll have to look for another job, she thought as she sank into the lounge.

Blake sat heavily next to her. "I've told my mother everything. I told her that I was responsible for what Mona did due to my being neglectful."

Olive opened her mouth to speak, but Blake continued, "I've righted my wrongs. I will tell Leo the truth of the matter when he is old enough."

"Why are you telling me all this? I'm just the nanny."

"There's a saying, and I don't know if you've heard it; you don't know what you've got 'til it's gone. I had a family; I had everything and I didn't value it; now it's the only thing that I want." Blake sat a little closer to Olive. "I want to be a better man for you, Olive. You're a genuine person and I want Leo and I to have that in our lives. I want to be the best man I can be for Leo, and with you beside me I know it will happen."

"Me beside you?" Olive frowned.

"Come on that date with me, Olive?"

Olive wanted to scream yes. She wanted more than anything to go on a date with him and if he were Amish she would have said yes, but he was not. "You know I can't, Blake."

"And why is that?"

"You aren't Amish."

"And if I were?"

Olive smiled at him and then looked down at her

hands in her lap. "Then I'd happily go on a date with you."

"Then, how do I go about becoming Amish?"

Olive looked up into his eyes and no words came to her for a moment. Had she heard correctly? "How do you become Amish?"

He nodded. "How do I go about that?"

Olive giggled. "You'd change your whole way of life for me to go on a date with you?"

"Not just a date. I would hope for more, of course. I would want us to marry."

Olive studied his face to see if he was joking. He surely couldn't be serious.

"I'm determined to be the best man I can be. Since I left God a long time ago, my life hasn't been right. He's calling me back to Him. He confirmed it when I saw you standing there the very first day you came to work for me."

"Ah, was that why you had such a temper toward me?"

Blake smiled. "I was running away from God's call on my life. I guess I might have been resisting

Him and taking it out on you." Blake flicked his eyes up to the ceiling and said, "Everything clicked for me when you told me about your childhood. I want Leo to have the best life possible. I miss having a family, a proper family. There's something I haven't told you yet; I paid a visit to your bishop on Saturday afternoon."

"You did?"

Blake nodded. "We had a long talk. I have respect for your bishop; he's an insightful man."

Olive stared into his face and wondered if he was joking. "What did he say?"

"I found out what I have to do to join the Amish."

Olive blew out a deep breath. *Was this really happening?*

"I won't disappoint you; I'm a changed man."

This was everything for which she had hoped.

"You know, the bishop said that it would be at least six months before we could court. Will that be long enough for you to learn to like me enough to court you?" Blake asked

Olive wanted to tell him exactly how she felt but

instead, she asked, "What does your mother say about all this?"

"My mother approves of anything that involves you. That's why she's agreed to watch Leo for the day. I'm determined to prove myself to you."

Olive stared at him open-mouthed.

"Olive, I'm a practical man. All I'm asking of you is one date before I join the Amish. Leo and I will have to live with a family for three months. It will be another three months before I'm able to court you, so that's six months at least before I can prove myself worthy. Will you have lunch with me today before I embark on that journey?"

"So you've decided to join us? You really want that?"

"Yes. Come to lunch with me and we'll talk about it?" Blake asked once again

Olive looked into his pleading dark eyes and smiled. "Alright, I guess one lunch couldn't hurt. But, only if we are clear that it is not a date; it's just a lunch."

He put a strong arm around her and hugged her

close.

She looked at him and asked, "Does this mean I'll be losing my job?"

He wrapped his other arm around her and held her tight. "You'll be getting much, much more. That is if you will want me in six months' time?"

Olive looked into his dark eyes and sent a silent prayer of thanks to *Gott* for answering her prayers better than she could have ever hoped.

When she did not answer him, Blake said, "You'll have time to get used to the idea of marrying me, and I'll have time to be the person I was meant to be."

Olive knew that he was just like his mother and would not take no for an answer. Smiling Olive said, "Everything always turns just the way in which it was meant."

* * * The End * * *
* * * * * * * * * * * * * * * *

Book 2 in the *'Amish Maids'* series OUT SOON

If you enjoyed *Choosing Amish* you might enjoy other books by Samantha Price
#1 BEST SELLING
'Amish Romance Secrets' series:

A Simple Choice: Book 1

When Kate was 14, the 19-year-old Benjamin promised to marry her when she was old enough.

Yet a few years later, Kate finds that Benjamin has married another Amish woman. Why did the honorable Benjamin go back on his word and marry someone else?

Kate's faith is shaken, and she vows to leave the Amish as soon as she is able.

After four years living in the *Englisch* world, Kate feels neither Amish nor *Englisch.*

To make matters worse, living away from the community and away from Benjamin has done nothing to lessen Kate's feelings for him.

Kate asks God to grant her a husband, yet never in her wildest dreams could she have imagined the way in which this unfolds.

Annie's Faith: Book 2

Annie is determined to win the handsome Jessie Yoder's heart.

The only thing standing in Annie's way is Liz, a long-term houseguest of Annie's family.

Annie is downcast, as Jessie cannot take his eyes off Liz.

Liz is everything that Annie is not.

While Annie wears plain clothes and no makeup, Liz wears the latest English fashions and is never seen without makeup or high heels.

Things go from bad to worse when Liz appears to be returning Jessie's attentions.

How can Annie possibly compete with the beautiful Liz to win Jessie's heart while staying true to her Amish values?

A Small Secret: Book 3

When Sarah falls in love with John, an *Englisher,* she is momentarily drawn away from her faith. When Sarah discovers she is having John's child, she attempts to hide her shame from the community.

John professes his love for Sarah through his letters, but when he doesn't send for her as promised, Sarah decides to keep the baby a secret from him.

She sets out to make a life for herself and her baby.

Sarah finds out first hand about God's forgiveness as she sees her life transform in a way she never thought possible.

Ephraim's Chance: Book 4

Ephraim has fallen in love with Liz. However, Ephraim's mother has other ideas and sets about for him to marry Ruth, a good Amish girl.

Liz is heartbroken and fears that not even returning to the Amish will be enough to win Ephraim's mother's approval. Ephraim decides to go against his controlling mother's wishes, but has he left things too late?

Ephraim discovers that a handsome, rich doctor is pursuing Liz. Ephraim fears that even if he is successful in his bid to win Liz, his secret might be enough to lose her forever.

A Second Chance: Book 5

True love does not strike twice in one lifetime - that is what fifty three year old Rebecca thought until she met the Amish man, Jeremiah.

While Rebecca contemplates her baptism and return to the Amish, her late husband's niece, Morgan, lands on her doorstep.

Rebecca tries to help the troubled teenager sort out her problems, but Jeremiah has very different ideas about how this should be achieved.

Will the relentless aggravation of this rebellious teen and the constant reminder of the intense love that Rebecca had for her late husband be enough to drive away Jeremiah?

Will Rebecca's desire to help her niece lose her a second chance at love?

Choosing Amish

Morgan, a tattooed girl with a past, and Amish man Jacob, have fallen in love. Having been caught up in a whirlwind romance, neither one of them has faced what is now standing between them.

One of them must choose to leave their past life behind them in order to create a life together.

Knowing that Jacob's sisters have found out about her past, Morgan wonders if Jacob's family will ever accept her.

Will Jacob leave the only life he has ever known as well as his faith for an uncertain future in the English world to be with Morgan?

Other Amish series by
Samantha Price
'Amish Secret Widows' Society'

The Amish Widow: Book 1
Hidden: Book 2
Accused: Book 3
Amish Regrets: Book 4
Amish House of Secrets: Book 5
Amish Undercover: Book 6
Amish Breaking Point: Book 7
Plain Death: Book 8

Other **#1 BEST SELLING** series
by Samantha Price
'Amish Twin Hearts' series:

Trading Places: Book 1
Truth Be Told: Book 2
Finding Mary: Book 3
Worlds Apart: Book 4

Also a **#1 BEST-SELLING** series-
'Amish Wedding Season' series
by Samantha Price:

Impossible Love: Book 1
Love at First: Book 2
Faith's Love: Book 3
The Trials of Mrs. Fisher: Book 4
A Simple Change: Book 5

****

Short Stories by Samantha Price:
'Single Amish Romance Short Stories'
series by Samantha Price:

The Other Road
The Englisher Girl
Amish Runaway Bride
Amish Love Interrupted
The Middle Son

Connect with Samantha Price at:
samanthaprice333@gmail.com
http//twitter.com/AmishRomance

Made in the USA
San Bernardino, CA
18 March 2015